IN THE TRENCHES

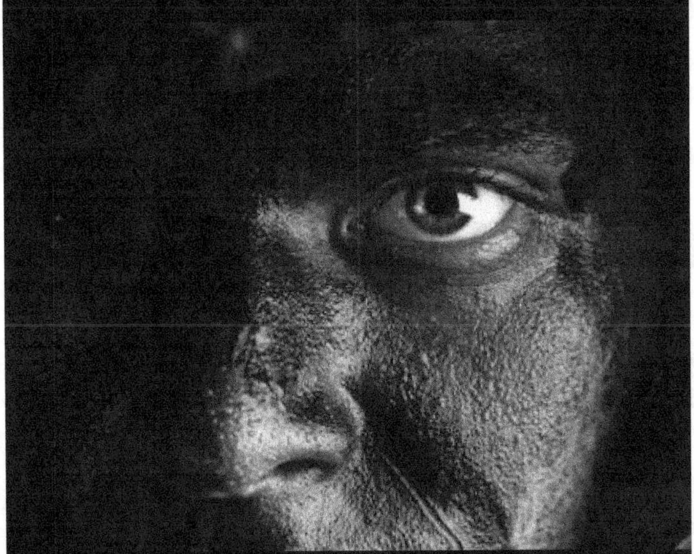

THE PSYCHOLOGICAL IMPACT OF WAR

In the Trenches:

The Psychological Impact of War

Book © Verto Publishing 2015

http://www.vertopublishing.com/
https://www.facebook.com/vertopublishing
Twitter: @vertopublishing.com

ISBN-13: 978-0692479933
ISBN-10: 0692479937

Edited and compiled by Krista Clark Grabowski

Assistant Editors L. E. Fitzpatrick and Elisha Murphy

Cover design © John D. Stanton

Contents

"In the Trenches" is about wars spanning history and taking place all over the world. Killing without mercy, bodies blown to bits before your eyes; physical and mental devastation. Peer into the heart, mind, and soul of a soldier during active duty and beyond. War forever changes men and women, and impacts everyone around them See through their eyes. View the horror of combat. See how it plays out when they come home to family and friends.

--Krista Clark Grabowski

John De Herrera

Untitled Prose Poem

What is it you would see? If it be woe or wonder, cease your search, and let the following be told to the unknowing world how these things came about--of carnal and bloody acts, of accidental judgments, casual slaughters, of deaths put on by cunning, and plans of deceit fallen upon the deceiver's heads. All this can truly be delivered, so let it be told, even while minds are wild, these words for the ear to make us dumb; let us recount the occasion of our sudden and strange return lest more plots and errors of mischance occur.

Oh how stale, flat and without purpose the world appears-- a garden gone to seed, weeds rank and gross possess it. That it should come to this, rendered beasts in comparison to gods of the sun we are meant to be--must we remember?

Some say 'tis but our fever, this dreaded sight that fills us with fear and wonder--this specter that appears when the stars have made their course to light the parts of heaven where they now burn. Do not break, our altogether heart, and sinews, grow not old, but bear us stiffly up, for we must hold until from dreadful secrecy the dreadful secret is known--until the apparition appears no more upon the battery where we watch.

We would not have believed it, this strange eruption in our state. So much brass going to cannons, ships being built seven days a week--what threat and purpose accounts for all this sweaty haste day and night? Who can answer the question of these wars? 'Tis a mote which troubles the mind's eye, for when Rome was high and triumphant before it fell, they say graves opened up and the shrouded dead went shrieking through the streets. Stars with trails of fire, disasters in the sun, the watery moon sick almost to doomsday with eclipse--harbingers of fates coming on-- such feared events do heaven and earth demonstrate to us now.

'Tis very strange, give it an understanding but no tongue. All is not well, this foul play, and these foul deeds will rise even though this original lie would overwhelm them to our eyes. Oh angels and ministers of grace do not let we who delight in truth as much as life itself burst from a lack of understanding, but tell why this specter has been cast up again. What does this mean, this visitation shining by the light of the moon--making night hideous and we fools of nature--shaking us with thoughts beyond the reaches of our souls. Oh say why this is--our fate cries out and makes each petty artery as hardy as the lion.

Caught round in a net of villainies, sorting the plot and play through to the end, is it not damned to let this canker come to further evil? We must defy the fear when examples evident as earth exhort us. We put on our antic disposition- -God's jester--while putting up with the calamities, bearing the whips and scorns of time, the injustice of tyrants, the arrogance of authorities, the law's delay--we bear these ills rather than fly to others that we know not of. Consciousness makes cowards of us all! Were these bones begotten for no better purpose than to be used for playing games? We are no more than sheep and calves to think a document of law alone will secure us. Do we stand in its way even though it would blast us? Where is this knowledge, which our knowing would help a fate avoid?

We're asked to cast off our melancholy and look upon the rule with kindness, for the excuse that everything passes through nature into eternity. Yet is it not an offense to heaven, the dead, and nature, to subvert this potential so? Our woe is yet to be proved of no avail--oh heaven direct our course, that we, with wings as swift as thinking and thoughts of love may sweep to our revenge; for the power of beauty will sooner transform honesty from what it is, than honesty could ever translate beauty into its likeness; and in the corrupted currents of this world the gilded hand may shove justice aside, as 'tis often seen, the wicked prize itself buys out the law. But 'tis not so in heaven above: there, there is no shuffling, no trickery, there every action lies in its true nature and we ourselves are compelled from the teeth to the forehead of our faults to give evidence in all.

But who comes to chide our tardiness? Do we not have the bile to make oppression bitter? Is this late visit but to whet our almost blunted purpose? Let us confess ourselves to heaven, repent what's past so we may avoid what is to come in times as obscene as these, where virtue itself begs the pardon of vice--bows and begs to do what is right.

This rule, whom we trust as we would fanged serpents, bears its mandate to sweep our path and marshal us to our doom. So be it--'tis sport to have the engineer blasted up with their own bomb. And it shall go, but we will delve one yard below its mines and blow it to the moon. Oh 'tis most sweet when in one line two schemes directly meet; oh that from this time forth our thoughts be bloody or nothing worth--where not even the ocean overpowers the flats with more haste than our rebellion sweeps it aside, as if the world begins now, former order be damned. Our state cries so loud to be heard, from heaven to earth, that we must question it all--and where the offence is, let a great axe fall.

Oh treble woe fall ten times treble on the cursed head whose wicked deed deprives us of our most fine sense. A desperate disease requires a desperate remedy for relief or there is none at all.

Whose grief bears such an emphasis, whose words of sorrow would cause the wandering stars to stand still like a wonder-struck audience? Humanity. And what a piece of work--how noble in reason, how infinite in ability, in form and movement--how exact and admirable--in action how like an angel, in apprehension, how like a god--the beauty of this world--we will fight until our eyelids no longer blink. Our skills shall indeed stand out like the most fiery star in the darkest of nights.

Perhaps heaven has pleased itself with us, that we may be its minister and scourge. Then venom to its work, and let it be known the moment will arrive where all shall appear as clear to judgment as day to the eye.

Suzanne Rancourt

Venom, Sweet Venom

Who are you?
A lover drowned by ego? A husband? A river?
Oh, fragrant pain moistened dew of desire to be something
you were afraid of becoming.

If I didn't know better I would think you never existed
but for the petaled-bruised magnolia flesh that could not
be touched
the oxidation of swirls and whorls of fingerprints rising up
to the surface, proof, that touching of some kind occurred
in your
crazy, confused life.

My sorrowful bucket gut roils with questions: who are you
in this moment
telling people a piece of the story like serving a slice of pie
but never the whole pie.
Only in moments of recollections can the wholeness be
reassembled
with the pulling of each berry seed, hull, and stem from
teeth, palette, and throat.
Fragments. Together. Apart. Together. Apart.

You were a flower
whose euphoric fragrance was as hypnotic and numbing as
a spider bite.
I emptied myself
into your poison.

Eric Paul Shaffer

April Fool: A Minor Event on L-Day, April 1, 1945, Okinawa

with no apologies to history

A perfect day for an invasion, blue sky, calm sea, high tide,
> a swift force at dawn takes an undefended
> beach:
men tense, shoulders hunched, stumble through
surf
> into Japan, without firing a shot.

"April fool," whisper waves on empty beaches,
"So far for so little."

> Two air fields occupied without opposition: the
> runways
> > change hands without a gesture of
> > defiance,
conquered so quickly, not everyone gets the word.
> Okinawa glints green and familiar from the
> air.

"April fool," soldiers grin ruefully over smokes
and rifles at rest.

At noon, a lone Japanese plane circles the field once
> and descends to the narrow dirt
> strip:
> a perfect landing in the last airfield he ever
> chose.

Americans stare as the plane taxies to the nearest
squad.
"April fool," whisper waves on empty beaches,
"So far for so little."

The pilot leaps from the cockpit and trots over. Only in his
last step
does the man see his mistake. A phrase of
amazement
escapes his lips, his eyes comic zeroes of
wonder.
Nobody speaks his language, and somebody shoots
him.

Eric Paul Shaffer

Voice of Stone: June 16, 1996, Peace Day on Okinawa

for #30571

The dead have forgotten us,
but we cannot forget them.

This hot June day, we number rocks
to touch the dead fifty years gone--
200,000 in a single season.
Some call that a battle.

Sea, sand, grass, stone, sun.

We stack stones, pile them singly
by the thousands,
hefting the dimensions of a loss
grown vague in a waste of days.

Stone by stone, we discover the work
in writing on rock. The natural resistance
of the material dulls the point,
clots the ink with dust.

The labor is not lost on us--
how much harder to die on such a day?

Sea, sand, grass, stone, sun.

The elements are fierce here. Life
grows swiftly among glaring immensities,
and none wish for more than shade,

water, a little laughter.

The traffic blurs, close and quick,

but the blare of horns
is crushed beneath a high, heavy sky,
lost in heat and green.

What we hear is the first summer cicada
whirring in limbs overhead.

Sea, sand, grass, stone, sun.

I picture one whose number I am
writing on rock: 30571.
With a single feature, a scent, one syllable
of a name now lost,

I want to say I remember
one I never knew,
but in the sun I see today
what is eternal is gone.

Sea, sand, grass, stone, sun.

On a still, searing day of peace,
grief at the immutable drives us
to choose a pen
to ink black figures on stone

for the unknown, across a broad green field
bound by a deeper blue than sky.
On a horizon receding only from us,
the lost remain, changeless,

faceless, diminished in a distance of days,
named now only with a number.

J. J. Steinfeld

Streets Are Not Always for Walking

I remember walking miles but I fail to remember my
destination or from where I had departed, only that I had
to walk and possessed no choice as to where I was going.
The last incident I can clearly recall from before the
walking is being in a small room with a woman who
showed me an old photograph of a young man in a military
uniform. She said to me, "This is your great-grandfather,
before he went off to war." After and before that
recollection everything is hazy except for the forced
movement. During my walk, at least initially, I did not
experience fear, worry, or even curiosity; I was too
smothered in the helplessness of my walking to give any
consideration to my plight. I simply moved in the direction
I had to move. I tried to listen to the sound of my footsteps,
but there was no sound, just the imprisoning silence.

Early during my walking on the concrete streets, I
mistakenly believed I was not being pulled or drawn. I
moved about the streets but was unable to find any familiar
sights or landmarks. I continued to walk, seemingly of my
own strength, and found myself making circles around the
quiet, empty city, or whatever one would call the area I was
in. My feeling of aloneness grew with each silent breath
and blind step.

The faster I walked, the more trapped I felt, little
different than an insect fighting to escape a spider's web. I
soon began to feel oppressive fear, worry, and trembling
curiosity. While thinking about the old photograph of the
young man in the military uniform, questioning whether
he was really my great-grandfather, I realized I did not
know who I was. Bad enough I did not know where I was or

where I had been, but who was I? I had been walking for hours and yet I had not once questioned my identity. How totally absurd, I thought, nothing but sheer madness.

I remembered the woman handing me the old photograph, the softness of her hand as I touched and held it, and her talking to me briefly, but nothing further. My life, for however long that had been, had become a mystery with only a few isolated shreds of remembrance left to me.

I craved a mirror to see how I looked, to determine if I was young or old, handsome or ugly, the colour of my skin. If the uniformed man in the photograph was my great-grandfather, then I must be white also. I looked at my hands to confirm my deduction and found I was wearing heavy gloves I had never seen. Trying to pull the gloves off proved futile and unnerving. I was unable to remove any of my clothing and there was no ready way to discover answers to the questions concerning my physical self.

Then I became aware there were no houses or buildings, or anything else that makes a city a city, in sight. There were only the endless streets and the noiseless air and the countless, perplexing questions. But foremost was my concern over who I was. I could form no mental picture of my parents or grandparents, of anyone in my family except the uniformed man who was supposed to have been my great-grandfather. I wished more than anything I was back in the small room with the woman who had shown me the old photograph, where she could answer my questions and protect me from the nightmare I was undergoing. I was sure of only one thing: I was not asleep.

It was neither day nor night around me as I walked, but a muted brightness that remained unchanging. I walked for what I estimated to be several days, possibly a full week, and not once was there a noticeable change in the time of day. On top of my other bafflements, I realized I could smell nothing, despite what I determined to be massive clouds of smoke or dust not far off in the distance. Perhaps more confusing was that I felt no hunger or fatigue, and I must have taken hundreds of thousands of steps since I had begun walking.

All of a sudden, I had the urge, for no apparent reason, to stop my senseless walking and find out how senseless standing still would feel. But my sudden, fierce desire went unfulfilled, and my already thick frustration grew more dense.

After a thousand more steps I was no longer walking; still moving, but not what one would call normal, one-step-after-another walking. I was moving by means of a blend of hopping, stumbling, and staggering. It produced an exhilarating feeling but still I wished I could stop, if just for a second or two, to convince myself I was capable of non-movement. I speculated I was trapped in some ghastly amusement-park ride or was a resident in a huge lunatic asylum in which the inmates are kept moving in order to make them harmless. What ludicrous, far-fetched notions, I scolded myself. No matter what, I told myself, I must not think like a fool or a madman.

More hours of forced movement passed before I began to feel tired for the first time since beginning my walking, and then in a matter of seconds I felt complete exhaustion. I could no longer delude myself that I retained some small control over my movement. I wanted to rest, to drop to the ground and not move, but was unable to slow my pace even a fraction. I attempted to scream, moving my lips desperately, but the only sounds I heard were inside me.

On and on I moved, the hopping-stumbling-staggering movement becoming more pronounced. I tried to close my eyes but that too was impossible. Control of my body had been stolen from me. I was confident of nothing and feared an eternity of this helpless existence. Fantasies of suicide occupied me. But how? How could I possibly kill myself when I could not do a simple act such as stopping. I was being victimized, but for what possible reason or purpose? Questions raged, but the answers were silently hidden away from me.

Without success, I attempted to devise some method for telling time. I could not even conjure up a guess as to how long I had been existing in this world of endless concrete streets. I could not say with any certainty if I had been walking for a month or years, or worst of all, for a few seconds. To save my mind, I convinced myself I was existing in a timeless world where walking was the sole important activity, and seconds, minutes, and hours—those created beasts of measurement—were meaningless, in fact, nonexistent.

So I continued to walk in my timeless, peopleless, buildingless world—what else could I do—wondering not only who I was, but also if I were getting older. Nonsense, I told myself, how can I get older if there is no time. I would have gained some relief if I could have laughed at the silliness of my logic, but could not make even a weak chuckle. My face, however constructed or shaped, was unwilling to allow anything faintly resembling a smile or laugh onto its sacred terrain.

"Got ya by the short hairs, don't we..." Out of nowhere, but loud and clear, came this idiotic statement. The words came from all sides, above and below me, from everywhere. I could not say if the words had been uttered by one voice or many in unison. Then, after the seventh or eighth time the stupid words had been repeated, laughter began to resound all around me. At first I thought it was a man laughing, later changing my opinion and deciding it was a woman. Still changing my mind another time and feeling the loud laughter belonged to a boisterous child. Man, woman, child?—I did not know who or what was

13

laughing at me. I did know the laughter was unlike anything I had ever heard before or, for that matter, ever wanted to hear again. Was one person or many laughing at me now? Was there any sound at all? Oh my mind...my wretched, pounding mind.

After what seemed like an eternity the laughter stopped and once more I found myself embedded in silence. What was worse, I asked myself, the silence or the insane laughter? I could not begin to answer.

I hopped-stumbled-staggered through countless more eternities of silence and senseless walking, every so often making a vain effort to form words or sounds, wishing I could sleep or die—it hardly mattered which. During a brief period of counterfeit peacefulness, the peculiar voice began to speak to me again.

"How have you been enjoying your fun-filled journey so far? Please don't attempt to answer because we still haven't decided to return your vocal powers to you. If we returned control too soon you would destroy yourself. Keep struggling away and we'll speak to you later. Remember, do not go smoking on Churchill's cigar...do not go sitting on Roosevelt's wheelchair...and do not, whatever you do, go growing Hitler's moustache..."

I did not know what the voice was talking about. Before I could make the slightest sense of the words or names, the rollicking, genderless, skull-penetrating laughter resumed. It was the same loudness as before, but this time had a sinister quality to it, or so I felt. Had there been any laughter in the first place? Yes! Certainly! But my answers were as ludicrous as my questions. I was a crazed dog chasing his tail. *Churchill's cigar, Roosevelt's wheelchair, Hitler's moustache...* What did it mean, what the hell did it mean?

I walked for countless more silent, tiring eternities, unable to rest or collapse, and tried to speculate, futilely of course, on what was happening to me. I was given almost entirely to brooding and self-pity. There seemed to be no escaping from my concrete maze, no return to wherever I had come from, but did I really want to return to some unknown prior existence? Perhaps where I had come from was a worse maze than the one I was now trapped in. Impossible! Preposterous! Nothing could be worse than all this endless, silent concrete.

I was made to run at a furious speed, once more unable to control my pace or movement. I was exhausted, painfully exhausted, but still could not slow down a step. "When will this all end?" I wanted to scream out loud; my thoughts could barely whisper the words.

As I was pulled by some unseen magnet, my body feeling like a hollow, drained effigy of clanking armour, I sounded a dainty burp. I felt great joy spread through my being. A sound, an actual sound had emanated from me, and it was as if I had just scaled the steepest cliff or done something as unbelievable as walk on water. Unbelievable?—of course not; I had just walked on the most torrential of waters. *I had burped.* There was no doubt about it, there was no denying my accomplishment. I had made a sound: a beautiful, mellifluous burp.

But only one? Was I allowed only one precious sound? I concentrated all my energy—however slight—on performing another burp. Lacking the ability to resist, my speed was altered to freakish slow motion but my obsessive quest remained: I still had to burp again.

I felt caught in a distorted version of a whirlpool, my mind and body trapped, forced to participate in a revolving, dizzying dance, a mangling of steps and rhythm. I was being spun, sometimes slowly, other times fast, a human top, a child's toy. My mind now seemed to spin in an opposite direction from my body. One second I felt I was standing erect, the next upside down, vertical and diagonal positions indiscriminately attacking my flesh. My tormentors were relentless. Humming and buzzing and ringing sounds filled the air around me, then once again the silence devoured all sound. The desire to make another burping sound left me altogether.

I experienced dizziness and motionless ecstasy; I felt the vibrancy of gentle movement and the stupor of laboured steps; I felt my skin being ripped and my weary bones caressed. Varied sensations reverberated through my body. Later, with the same abruptness as the whirlpool motion had begun, it ceased, and I was thrust again into my prison of hopping-stumbling-staggering movement. I now began to remember people and places, but not names or geographical locations. My memory was defiant of chronology and nomenclature, yet I was recalling episodes from my life, even though they were jumbled. It was like seeing objects plainly beneath the surface of limpid water, but not knowing what those objects were. No matter what, it was still life-affirming memory.

Memory and movement became more mixed; colours and sounds interchanged. With a stinging suddenness I started to experience smell, and the only smell was of smoke. I felt numbed by fever and melted by cold; I felt damp and dry, unsteadily weak and powerfully strong. It was as if my senses were going berserk. Then I was frozen into a standing position.

My senses cleared and my mind relaxed, but my body remained rigid. I was unable to control one muscle, to move a single segment of my anatomy. Still another confusing slap at my life. How long could I remain unmoving? Earlier I had wanted non-movement; now I loathed it as much as the movement. A common factor strangled both the movement and non-movement: I had no control over my body.

I became more frightened than ever as I was forced to remain still, unblinking, doubting my attachment to life.

The scene before me became a thick, sombre mist hovering above an ocean of lifeless concrete. I created imaginary characters and carried on lengthy conversations with them in my mind. I assumed many roles and played at many games. But how does a statue occupy an eternity?

I tried to follow the procession of memories racing through my mind, but they became too swift, too disconnected. I wanted to abandon myself to crying—a baby can cry—but I was being denied the comfort of emotional release. My prisons were multiplying, taking on new and crueller forms. I could not begin to plan my escape—my prisons were everywhere; I was living in incarceration.

Suddenly the misty atmosphere brightened; colours flashed vividly and distinctly: oranges, blues, greens, reds. The colours of fire. The smell of smoke grew. My body shivered and soon I experienced the pleasure of a shaking fit. How ridiculous to enjoy an uncontrollable fit, but it was a different movement and it was invigorating. The shaking fit ended abruptly and I was returned to my rigid position.

I remained rigid, with no indication I would ever be allowed to move. When I was nearly resigned to an existence of non-movement, I was forced to walk, much in the same manner as when I first found myself in this unknown place. Perhaps everything around me was proper, in good order, as it should be. Was I so improper, so out of order? I could arrive at no conclusions, make no judgments. I could think of nothing as certain or definite.

Finally I felt tears, the dew of emotion warming my cheeks. What a saving show of humanity. I was crying and that was important. I no longer cared if I was moving or not, that I was being tormented and controlled. I had discovered an inner peace, some sense within the madness.

The tears ceased. The inner peace dissipated. I tripped and fell harshly to the ground. My body, face down, was forced against the concrete and I experienced still another prison. When I felt blood in my mouth I was not frightened; it was more proof of my humanity, and I savoured the taste. A person bleeds, a person reacts when hurt, and I was bleeding.

Soon there were no smells, no sounds, no colours, no tears, only prostrate captivity, the affirmation of blood. So what...so damn what. It just did not matter anymore.

"Do not be sad. Whatever you do, do not give up. Churchill never gave up. Roosevelt never gave up. Hitler, we must acknowledge, did give up. You have a vast distance to go. We might say your journey is at the beginning."

Silence. An immeasurable period of time elapsed. A second? An hour? A century? I could not decipher the names this time either. At last the voice continued.

"As a gesture of our generosity, we will return your power of speech. We will also permit you to stand up. What do you say to that, our friend?"

Like a marionette being pulled upright, I was jerked to a standing position. There was a looseness to my posture, not rigidity as before. Then without any thought or hesitation, I exploded into speech: "You bastards, tell me what the hell's going on and where the hell—" I continued to move my lips but words failed to sound.

"You have abused our generosity and now you must be punished. You have lost your privilege of speech again," the peculiar voice said, no emotion in its tone.

Blood rushed to my head as I found myself placed upside down on the concrete, a position that was most distasteful. Pretending not to care about myself, pretending to be indifferent to my plight, was useless. I was enraged. The more I experienced helplessness and frustration, the angrier I became. But what could I do? My head felt leaden, my body enervated. When will this all end? When? When? When?...

Time seems to go slower when you are upside down. I look forward to fainting, to experiencing the comfort of unconsciousness, but I know not even restful blankness will be given to me. Once more I became desperate with concern as to who I was, where I was, whether I existed. I told myself I was alive, existing, by the very fact that I was thinking of such words as *alive* and *existing*. The arguments were simple and unoriginal, and they did not satisfy me. Could I be dead? How was I to know how death felt? How was I to know anything? My own thoughts terrified me. Of course I was not dead! But what was I? What words could I give to my situation, to my existence? I realized the idiocy of my thoughts, yet I could not expel them.

As I was searching my memory for clues to my identity, I found myself walking at an easy, unhurried pace. I was still walking on the concrete streets, but no longer hopping-stumbling-staggering, and the scene before me began to change. Further confusion, deeper mystery, however pleasant and welcome the change. Hills and rivers and canyons appeared, disappeared and reappeared, flowing through an unsteady landscape. Everything within my view was in flux, changing colours and shapes. Shadowy mists and bright colours played randomly across my range of vision. I tried to catalogue what I was seeing, to make sense of my surroundings, but leaping to the sun would have been more possible.

The colour of the sky became the colour of the small room I had once been in. The room where I first saw the old photograph of the young man who was supposed to have been my great-grandfather. Sensing the woman who had shown me the photograph was near, I wanted to call for her, but what name could I give? I did not know if she was a stranger or lover, my sister or mother.

A symphonic mixture of unknown and recognizable sounds greeted me, then departed quickly; silence and laughter alternated. The laughter became louder, less bearable. I whispered a few words to determine if I could still speak, and discovered a bland joy in saying, "When will this all end?"

My movement stopped and I was allowed to stand still in a comfortable manner. I felt someone stroking the back of my head tenderly. It was not long until I was being stimulated by a moist tongue moving slowly over my neck. The sensation was not foreign to me; it brought back the memory of past pleasures. I prayed that behind me was the woman who had shown me the old photograph. My mind reconstructed her room to the tiniest detail.

Without warning my body was twisted around and I saw corpses, all of them burned. I could not tell if they had been male or female; there were more corpses than I could count in a hundred years. I started to beat at my face. I was gripped in such an insane frenzy that I did not immediately realize I had control over my hands. *I* was striking at my face.

The corpses disappeared. Laughter burst out all around me as my body shook with tears. I fell to the ground, at first swallowed in another shaking fit, and then becoming a weeping mass of beaten flesh.

Through my swollen, tearful eyes I looked up and saw human figures standing near me. The laughter did not seem to be coming from these figures, but from elsewhere, from innumerable other voices.

I screamed at the voices to shut up until I could no longer utter words. The laughter increased, a harsh rebuttal. My crying transformed into coughing and gagging. The coughing and gagging ended when a horrible new pain choked me into silence. I felt raw and torn apart, finally just empty.

Most of the laughter stopped. I took a few deep breaths, wetted my lips, and spoke: "What are you people doing to me?" I was unable to banish the echo of tears from my voice.

Each of the figures, one at a time, calmly asked, "Can't you take a joke?" But their mouths did not move. Then together the figures chanted the question over and over, later joined in concert by the voices from unseen people: "Can't you take a joke? Can't you take a joke? Can't you take a joke?..."

"Leave me alone!" I yelled, and then bit my lip as hard as I could to keep from beginning a curse I knew I would never be able to end.

Everything became silent, the dread quiet I remember from when I first began walking. I felt incredible agony. Nausea and agony, my skin burning.

The figures, still without moving their mouths, resumed speaking in one voice: "It is unfortunate you are so confused and upset. A human being should be able to take a little joke. You can speak, walk, cry—what more could you want?"

"Where was I taken from?" I moaned out. "Tell me how to return."

"You were never taken away," I heard the peculiar voice say, the words escorted through my mind by laughter.

Then I heard a single voice distinctly say, "He was the only one here to survive..." The voice and words were ordinary, unlike the laughter. I looked up and saw soldiers. I did not recognize the uniforms or type of breathing masks the soldiers were wearing over their faces. When I looked down, I saw I had on the same uniform as the soldiers, except that my uniform was burned and tattered and spotted with blood.

Another voice talked about giving me an injection to ease pain and I heard someone say they were preparing for another attack, but the words became fainter and fainter. My great-grandfather, I recalled, had died in a war. God, which war had *I* been caught in?

21

I closed my eyes and thought of the old photograph of the young man who had been my great-grandfather. I tried to think of which war he had gone off to fight. If I could remember my great-grandfather's war, perhaps then I would know who I was and what had happened to everything around me.

Donald Jacob Uitvlugt

Good Dog

When He whistles I wake
from dreams of chasing rabbits
through fields fresh with dew
and clover
to this stink of heat and dust
and men too close together.

I do not care; He is with me.

We hunt, He and I.
His eyes are sharp, but
my nose is sharper, sharp to smell
under the dirt, under the dust,
I smell the bad things, the metal things,
the things that are danger
to Him.

I bark, and He calls the good men,
the good men who come with their machines,
machines that destroy the bad things
in fire.

We hunt, and it is good.

But today the bad thing is
so deep
I do not smell it in time,
I do not smell the bad thing
and it bites.
With a thunder of fire, it bites.

23

With a crash of smoke, it bites.
With a hail of dirt, it bites.

It bites Him.

I whine and paw at His arm,
I bark and wag my tail,
I sniff and lick His face.
Above us sing the metal insects,
the metal insects the bad men send
to bite and hurt the good men.

We cannot stay here.

So I take His leg in my teeth
and I pull His leg with all my might.
He does not move and
I cannot move Him
and I wish, I wish just once
more
we were home
chasing rabbits.

The metal insects sing their whining songs,
they bite me and I do not care,
they sting me but they do not
sting Him.
I make sure of it.

He is my God. I cannot let Him die.

He groans and I whimper and nuzzle Him
and I do not smell the men
approach
until they are there.
Good, bad, I do not care.

They try to take Him from me and
I growl and show my teeth
until He opens
His eyes.

I go to Him
and lick His hand
and He smiles
and pats my head.

"Good dog."

So I let the good men take Him,
take Him into their den
where the good men will fix Him
while I lie here outside
and wait.

I wait, so tired.

So tired that I close my eyes
and wait for Him
to hunt rabbits
with Him
tomorrow...

"For my brother, and all who serve."

Donald Armfield

Hallucinating Yellow Sunshine

They fed us like animals.
Nourishment and rations on a stick.
Fused with yellow sunshine.

Our minds were elsewhere,
wandering through polluted thoughts.
The fields we traveled
terrains of dense grass, massive puddles.
Sinking in deep concentration

Lack of lethargy, blazing at first sight.
Instinct in the blink of the eye.
Trained trigger fingers,
to mutilate flesh at the drop of a dime.

Ruptured brain splatter,
bloodied graffiti, tainting the grounds.
A generated cemetery,
sowing the landscape with blood
within minutes.

Nowadays those faces, haunt our dreams.
Hallucinating flashbacks
the yellow sunshine that poisoned our minds.
Psychochemical warfare test monkeys,
replaying our feat, in vivid image.
Of the fallen who melted,
into the earth.
From the trajectory fire
our platoon spread that day.

Matthew Wilson

Waiting For The Dead

A good soldier keeps his feet dry
As he writes his letters home
Cupping shaking hands against his lighter
Deceiving things that nightly roam.

Silence is a soldier's safe line
Whispering jokes to help the mood
Shaking water from his bed at dawn
Picking lices from off his food.

Superstition weighs on these survivors
Kissing photos of their lady love
Squinting through choking yellow smog
From light the moon throws down above.

Soggy posters warn of talking
Between the bangs of mortar fire
Saluting as generals raise their swords
Farewell to fallen heroes on the pyre.

Alexis Liosatos

The Man Who Collected Dali

Gala slept soundly upstairs, while in the studio, a nightmare accumulated in oils. The house was silent. A single light burned in the darkness, illuminating the canvas as it received the final touches. Salvador Dali put down the brush, and stepped back to admire his work. Here it was, his vision given form, oil paints glistening like newborn flesh.

Dali narrowed his eyes before the lidless eyes of his creation. In the still house, under cold electric light, the effect was unnerving. He'd stalked this one for years, searching for its form, for its true face. He caught glimpses of it in Florence, Arcachon, Figueras and Port Lligat. And by degrees, Dali had come to realize *it* was stalking *him*. It had dogged him across the borders of Europe and taken its toll – friends killed in cold blood, family arrested and tortured. Dali fled the continent and did not sleep easily until there was an ocean between them.

He considered the smooth, sepia flesh, the knotted shoal of carrion worms, the honeycombed hollows of its eyes. It was strange how such nightmares had brought him everything – wealth, fame, adulation. And this was a vision as powerful as any he'd dragged into the waking world. Nothing could be added without diluting the purity of it. No trademark flourishes, no grasshoppers or soft watches.

Dali held out his right hand and turned it in the light. Then, with a slow, deliberate movement, he pressed his palm into the wet surface at the corner of the canvas. It was something he'd never done before, and he didn't know what had compelled him. He fumbled for a rag to wipe the paint from his hand. The handprint was clearly visible in the surface of the oils. It would be easy to paint it out, of course it would. No one need know it was there...but somehow, it was *right*. It belonged there. The superior artist knew not to over analyse his work. Too much of the rational kills the surreal. Perhaps the handprint was a seal, binding its spirit into the oil glaze.

It was done. Dali finished cleaning his hands and left the studio.

Buchner had never cared for Dali, or any of the modern, 'degenerate artists'. Even before the Führer had condemned them as such, and outlawed their work – Buchner had never liked it. He preferred simple, pastoral scenes. Art, to his mind, should depict a tranquil, restful idyll.

However, Buchner recognized Dali's talent, and hated to see his work destroyed like this.

The owner of this modest collection, Monsieur Veron, snuffling blood from his broken nose into a handkerchief, watched helplessly as his study was ransacked. It had been a bad day for Veron, and it was about to get worse. Framed pictures were ripped from walls and smashed on the floor. Shelves swept bare, artwork thrown in a heap among broken glass. A bureau was upended, papers cascading from drawers. A sketch of an elongated woman, her torso spilling drawers, fluttered to the floor and was trampled by a jackboot. The SS men were enjoying their work.

Buchner stood sheepishly to one side. He'd liked Veron. As Civilian Administrator to the Reich, he had even tried to protect him. When he learned of the raid, Buchner attempted to intervene. Veron's cache of forbidden art had been drunkenly revealed by his housekeeper, a local girl who whored herself to the SS for extra rations. But Buchner's authority did not extend over the SS, who would be satisfied with nothing less than dragging Veron to the Gestapo, who in turn would send him to the camps.

Assuming, of course, he survived this session of art criticism.

Buchner recognized a few artists among the illicit works heaped on the floor: Ensor, Beckmann, Dali, Dix. The latter two had proven especially problematic for Veron. SS-Sturmmann Drescher, a sharp-faced recruit, keen to impress his superiors, had discovered a print of Dali's *'Enigma of Hitler.'* It depicted the Führer menaced by a gigantic, melting telephone. Art criticism had rarely been so swift and incisive – Drescher clubbed Veron to the floor with a whipping backhand.

He'd barely clambered back to his feet, when Drescher became enraged by another print: Otto Dix's *'Seven Deadly Sins.'* Buchner thought it was well painted, but unfortunately for Veron, it featured a midget Hitler leading a parade of whores and freaks. Drescher's response was predictably savage. All things considered, Veron got off lightly with a broken nose.

For a just moment, Buchner caught his eye, and Veron managed a sad smile. He looked more resigned than frightened. In the years to come, Buchner would remember that expression and take cold comfort in it. It seemed to contain no accusation, no hatred – he hoped Veron understood that he had played no part in this.

Six months earlier, Buchner had spent a more pleasant afternoon with Veron. He'd been in good spirits. Buchner couldn't remember the last time a local had smiled at him. Perhaps Veron had enjoyed the benefit of the season's vintage over lunch. He looked dapper in a waistcoat, half-moon glasses, his grey moustache neatly trimmed. Buchner's business with Veron was masked as a polite social call. He wanted to assure him that although the previous administrator had retired in ill health, as his replacement, he would be running a tight ship.

Veron was a retired banker from Marseille, respected by the other villagers. A widower with no children, he was something of a solitary man. But during the panic as the Nazi occupation began, he'd managed to calm the villagers. As their unofficial spokesman, he'd helped to negotiate a semblance of normality during the uneasy co-existence with the Wehrmacht and the SS.

Ville-sur-Espérer was a small village with no more than ninety people. Many of the younger men were held as prisoners of war in Germany, leaving mostly women, children and the elderly behind. The village was of significance only because it was close to an important bridgehead. This strategic point was being reinforced against possible Allied attack.

To Buchner's mind it was an ungodly mess and a waste of more lives. The Nazi dream had ended and become a nightmare from which Germany could not awake. The shattering air raids. Stalingrad. The Kursk. The constant losses since...Buchner could see the war had already been lost. The Western Allies were marshalling their forces to invade France, and that would seal it. But Hitler would never surrender; not if every German city were reduced to scorched and skeletal ruins.

Veron impressed Buchner with his level-headed civility. Of course, beneath this veneer, he knew Veron hated him, his predecessor, and every last German stationed in France. However, he didn't hate *all* things German. Buchner recognized some of the artwork on his walls as that of German artists. There were etchings by Otto Dix and Max Beckmann, along with pieces by modern artists like Dali and Picasso.

"I'm afraid the Picasso is only a print," said Veron. "But I have etchings and even a few drawings in my humble collection."

"I'm surprised to see the work of German artists," said Buchner, studying the framed pictures.

"Ah. Well, *these* German artists are not respected in their homeland. Most of them have been branded 'degenerate' and expelled or forbidden to paint," Veron handed Buchner a small cup of coffee with a disarming smile.

Buchner was sure he'd never have spoken so candidly to his predecessor. Clearly, word had gotten around that he was a softer touch, and his stern posturing seen for what it was. These people had lived among the SS – they knew what ruthless bastards were *really* like. He took Veron's openness as a gesture of trust rather than insubordination.

"To be honest, they are not my favorite artists either," said Buchner "But between you and I...well, I dislike party policy in destroying art and burning books."

Veron laughed. "The party only destroys work it can't sell for a high enough profit. I have it on good authority that Goering came to Paris many times and helped himself to his favorite 'Degenerate Art.' The bonfire they had at Jeu de Paume was for leftovers they couldn't shift. It's all politics. None of it is about art, really. Now, my favorite is Dali. A few of his pieces went up in smoke during that big burn up."

"Dali can paint," said Buchner. "I'll give him that. I can see the skill in his work...but he's more of a showman. He courts controversy – and it works – it's made him a very wealthy man."

Veron nodded "Hm. *'Avida Dollars.'* Well, there's some truth in that. And I don't like all of his work myself. But we judge an artist by his *best* work, not his worst or some ill-defined average. And Dali's best work is...*visionary*. Let's see...yes, this one – *'Premonition of Civil War.'*" Buchner stepped forward and studied the reproduction; the barren desert, the colossal, fleshy monstrosity filling the sky, groping and clutching at itself.

"It's...ah...certainly *powerful*," said Buchner. "I can't claim to understand it, but it's a superbly painted nightmare."

Veron tapped the glass of the picture frame. "Well, this apparition represents Spain – look, it forms the outline of the country with its shape," he traced the geography across the glass with his finger. "And it's grasping at itself in a cannibalistic fervor. You see, Dali completed this piece just six months before civil war broke out. The grisly feast was about to begin."

Buchner swallowed the dregs of his coffee. "Alright...then this is *clever* as well as skillful. But I still don't like it. I give Dali his due, but I wouldn't hang this on my wall."

"We should be grateful for our artists," said Veron. "They perceive things we cannot. Their vision opens our eyes."

"Well, I prefer a good landscape painting. I love the colors and effects of light that your Impressionists capture. I can immerse myself – *lose* myself in a Monet or a Renoir."

Veron refilled their coffee cups. "If only," he said. "If only life were as pretty as Impressionist painting."

The SS decided it would be amusing to see Veron destroy his own collection. Drescher had shoved him to his knees and was barking at him to throw the artwork onto the open fire burning in the hearth. Veron hesitated. Drescher stabbed the toe of his boot into his ribs, the other SS men laughing. Hands trembling, Veron gathered a stack of artwork and stumbled to the fireplace. He bowed his head and dropped the pages into the flames. Buchner saw the etchings and drawings, the thoughts and visions of the artists char and catch light. One of Dali's burning giraffes reared and galloped up the chimney in a volley of sparks.

"And the rest!" shouted Drescher. "Throw all the degenerate Jew daubings into the fire!" Veron staggered back to the pictures on the floor, but the Frenchman, normally so composed, was coming apart at the seams. He fell to his knees, and scrambling to pick up the artwork, he cut his hand on a sliver of glass. But it wasn't the pain or

33

the blood that upset him. He stared at the picture on top of the stack, shaking his head.

The SS men laughed in guttural cacophony. "Come on, old man! Into the fire with them!" But Veron couldn't get up, he was sobbing over his drawings, staining them with blood and tears. Still laughing, Drescher unfastened his holster and reached for his pistol.

Buchner had seen enough. He didn't know if he was brave or stupid, but he went to Veron and knelt beside him. "Let me help you with these," he whispered, and gently took the pictures from his shaking hands. The laughter of the SS men ebbed into silence. The loudest thing in the room was the crackling of the fire as it devoured the artwork. Buchner stood up with the last of the drawings and walked to the fireplace. He dropped them into the flames and watched as they shriveled and burned.

The picture on top, the one Veron had cried over, was unmistakably a Dali, an original drawing by the look of it. It was probably the prize of Veron's small collection. It was also one of the most powerful and disturbing images Buchner had ever seen. It depicted a towering death's head with tiny, writhing human figures trapped inside its mouth and eye sockets.

It reminded Buchner of certain medieval woodcuts, depicting the Mouth of Hell, where sinners burned in eternal torment. But this was no dusty, ancient relic. The death's head seemed to be alive, gazing defiantly from the fire. The paper it was drawn upon rippled and blackened as it was swallowed by flames, but its after-image still glowed in the cinders, still smoldered in Buchner's brain. He rubbed his hand across his eyes, took a deep breath and turned to face the room.

Veron had been hauled to his feet and stood limply between two SS men, the firelight reflecting in his glasses. "I'm finished here," said Buchner "Do what you must." He brushed past Drescher and left the house, half expecting to be reprimanded or even shot. He turned and walked up the street, glad for the rain on his face to wash away the smell of burning. He heard the door to Veron's cottage slam shut and the sound of the SS vehicle starting. The open-backed truck drove towards him, but he kept his head down, kept walking. They sped past, and Buchner saw Veron for the last time, huddled in the back of the truck, jolted over the cobblestones, deathly pale among the black mass of the SS.

Now, more than ever, Buchner wanted the war to be over and to return home. The Allies had finally invaded France, and opened another front in the South of the country. They were pressing relentlessly forward: Toulon, Marseille and Paris were under attack and Buchner doubted the Wehrmacht could hold them for long.

It had come too late for Monsieur Veron. He'd been interrogated by the Gestapo and declared a political activist, a helper of the resistance. They sent him to one of the camps – to Buchenwald, Natzweiler or Dachau, somewhere into the *Nacht und Nebel,* where his chances of surviving the war vanished along with him. It was foolish, but Buchner felt responsible. If only he'd warned Veron to get rid of the artwork, or to hide it.

The Allied forces closed in upon Ville-sur-Espérer. The bridgehead had been fortified, and German troops stood ready to defend it. Buchner had arranged to evacuate the civilians to safety before the Allies made their move. Even the SS had raised no objections to this. Late one afternoon, with the fighting so close he could hear the thudding of distant artillery, Buchner was returning from the neighboring village where he'd finalized plans for the evacuation. None of this was required in his official duties to the Reich, and Buchner was drained and exhausted. The Allied forces would arrive within days now. You could see it in the eyes of every soldier, every villager – they sensed the approach of some great and final resolution.

As he left his car and turned towards his office, Buchner saw a small boy of about eight years old come running through a copse of trees. He recognized the child as one of the villagers. The boy was in such a panic he ran straight into Buchner.

"Steady on there," said Buchner, holding the boy by the shoulders "What's the problem? What mischief have you gotten into?" He tried to sound reassuring, but the boy was like a trapped animal. His eyes were wild and rolled heavenwards in sheer terror. The sight of him caused Buchner to loosen his grip, and the boy twisted free and tried to run again. Before he'd taken two steps, a gunshot cracked the afternoon air. The boy fell to the ground, like a puppet with its strings cut.

Drescher strode from the trees with his rifle. "Thanks for stopping him. That little bastard could run, alright." He barged past Buchner, slinging his rifle over his shoulder. Then he bent down and grabbed the dead boy by the scruff of his collar and dragged him through the mud, back toward the trees. It was a few seconds before Buchner could move or speak. "Wait!" he said, starting after Drescher "What – what the hell are you *doing?*" But Drescher carried on to the trees, dragging the small body behind him, the boy's hair blowing across his face like meadow grass. "You've murdered this child in cold blood!"

"So? You've been away for hours, neglecting your duties to the Reich. You're more concerned with these vermin than the war effort." As he spoke, Buchner heard sounds coming from the other side of the trees. Terrible sounds.

"What are you talking about? I've arranged it all...the evacuation. These are civilians – women and children! They'll play no part in the fighting!"

Drescher smiled, relishing Buchner's disorientation. "You shouldn't have gone to all that trouble, my friend. We've taken care of the evacuation for you."

They emerged from the copse of trees, into a world where everything had been turned inside-out. Into a world of pure, surreal horror. Just a few hours ago, Buchner had looked out upon a quiet village, with people going about their daily business. Under the hazy morning sun, it could have been a scene painted by Monet. But now, the little village had taken an appalling turn into nightmare.

The church was blackened and burning. Charred bodies hung out of the broken windows, where villagers had tried to escape the flames, only to be shot by the SS. Low moans and children's screams were punctuated by the crack of gunshots. In their uniforms, the SS men looked like black locusts, picking through the corpses, dispatching any survivors. An SS-Rottenführer strode solemnly in their wake, composing epitaphs in an elegant hand; slipping them into the pockets of the still-warm dead. The air stank of burning flesh and singed hair. Buchner stood in a landscape hell-black as a vision from Bosch or Goya.

"This is their punishment," said Drescher, shifting his grip on the dead boy. "Your precious villagers were helping the resistance. An SS convoy was attacked by partisans this morning. An officer and three good men killed. What did they *think* was going to happen? Did they think there would be no consequences?"

Buchner blinked hard against the horror and tried to speak, but the words died on his lips.

"We have to make an example of them." The evening sun glinted on Drescher's cap badge. He heaved the boy's corpse onto a pile of dead children and dusted off his hands. "We've got the Americans and British to worry about – we don't need these vipers biting us." The impact of the boy's body awakened a little girl lying among the corpses. Perhaps she was a classmate of the boy; her eyelids fluttered open and she shivered and gasped for breath. Drescher sighed wearily, pulled the rifle from his shoulder and aimed it, squinting down the iron sights, point blank into her face.

Buchner lunged forward and grabbed the gun, trying to wrest it from him. Drescher cursed as they struggled then glanced over Buchner's shoulder and smiled.

A rifle butt thudded into the back of Buchner's skull. He fell to his knees, then slumped face first into the mud. He couldn't think, couldn't speak; events swam in and out of focus, unfolding in languorous slow motion. Quite casually, Drescher took aim again at the little girl and pulled the trigger. The report of the gunshot deafened Buchner and something splattered across his face. Away. He had to look away from what Drescher had done.

Buchner's eyes lolled across a hellish, burning landscape with the living and the dead, the devils and the damned. Then, in this unearthly place, he saw something he had seen before. The church was no longer a church. It was now a towering, charred death's head, a monster that devoured the living. Its servants were the little death's heads...the black *Totenkopf* demons that pried open the doors and let the souls of the damned spill from its mouth.

Buchner lay in the dirt overnight and was found the next morning by a woman from the neighboring village. She recognized him as the official who'd tried to arrange the evacuation, and nursed him as well as she could. Once the bridgehead was captured, and the Allies had liberated the area, she handed Buchner over to them. He spent weeks in hospital with a fractured skull. By the time he'd recovered, the fighting in France was largely over, and the Allied war machine had rolled towards Belgium and Luxembourg as it pressed east for Germany.

Eighty-five civilians were murdered at Ville-sur-Espérer, the majority of them burned alive in the church. After the war, there was an investigation into the massacre and a trial. Many of the accused claimed they'd been conscripted *malgré-nous* into the SS, and were acquitted on these grounds. Even the convicted were imprisoned for just five years. Buchner himself was questioned about his conduct. He agreed with the prosecution that despite his position, he had helped to save nobody: not Veron, not the children, not even the little boy he'd held in his arms. Testimony from a neighboring villager cleared Buchner of all charges.

The SS were typically thorough in their liquidation of the village, and Ville-sur-Espérer was never repopulated or rebuilt. The charred ruins still stand today as a silent and slowly crumbling memorial. Only three residents survived the war; Monsieur Veron was not among them. He'd been moved from one concentration camp to another, and is believed to have died at Dachau, one of the many thousands of unregistered deaths there. *'Lieber Gott, mach mich dumm, damit ich nicht nach Dachau kumm.'* And perhaps, at his age, Veron didn't live to see that camp and its brutal guards, inhuman slave labor and epidemic typhus. He might have died during the forced march there. Or perhaps at the previous camp. Nobody could say. As the Gestapo had intended, he was lost in the *Nacht und Nebel,* in the night and fog.

Buchner returned to Germany, and found a job with a machine tool manufacturer in his hometown of Essen. The city had been devastated by Allied bombing and tens of thousands left homeless. Buchner was one of the lucky ones whose house had survived intact. Life was hard in the post-war ruins, shortages of food and fuel, strict rationing...Buchner found it best to throw himself into his work. Germany was on its knees and would need a strong manufacturing base if it were to drag itself from the rubble.

The spiritual ruins of Germany were more difficult to restore. The inhumanity of the Holocaust was put under the spotlight for all to see. Massacres that made Ville-sur-Espérer seem parochial in scale: At Rumbula in Latvia, the

SS shot dead 25,000 civilians. At Babi Yar in the Ukraine, almost 34,000 were murdered in cold blood. There could be no answers, no panacea for these things. Nowhere deep enough to neatly file them away.

But Buchner was determined to play his part in the rebuilding of Germany. Labor may not make us free, but it can serve as a powerful distraction. Work became his life, and he found little time for the art, books and music he used to enjoy. He lost touch with his few friends who had survived the war. It seemed easier that way – he could no longer summon the energy to invest in friendships.

Over the years, without wishing it, he'd drifted into a few romances that threatened to become serious. It had taken a surprising effort of will to starve the hope from these women. A decade crept by, and Buchner was still very much married to the company, albeit in a more senior position. He was now a representative, trusted to broker deals on the company's behalf.

One such business trip in the late summer of 1956 took Buchner into Belgium to secure a lucrative contract. The business was concluded in a satisfactory manner; but he was unable to get a train home until the following morning. He found himself with an evening to kill in the exclusive Flanders resort of Knokke. Spending nights alone in hotel rooms was nothing unusual for him. Normally he would have eaten in-house, read his newspaper and retired early for bed. But tonight was different.

For the first time in years, Buchner felt there might be something out there for him besides company business. He freshened up and left the hotel, deciding to try one of the restaurants along the sea front. The seafood was excellent, as was the wine; and he drank more than he might have normally. Stepping back out onto the street, Buchner was swept up in a crowd of people who were talking loudly and laughing. The women were too young for him, but beautiful, and it felt good to be in the presence of youthful cheer and optimism. Time was moving on – these people would have been children during the war. Perhaps with a new generation, the heavy aura of the war years was lifting.

But September on the Flanders coast was growing cold. A fog was rolling in from the sea, and Buchner decided to have one more drink before heading back to his hotel. The crowd of young revelers bustled into a large casino, designed in the modern fashion, but impressive nonetheless. It looked to be a popular spot, and Buchner thought it as good a place as any for his last drink. He followed the crowd inside, out of the chill night air. He had no intention of gambling, but bought a cognac from the bar, and wandered around, watching the people relax and have fun.

The casino was quite the pleasure palace, designed with no expense spared. Magnificent crystal chandeliers glittered over the gaming tables and spinning roulette wheels. Buchner was surprised the casino boasted its own art gallery. He'd never seen the like in any German casino, though admittedly it had been years since he'd been inside one. In fact, it had been years since he'd been inside an art gallery of *any* kind. Buchner hadn't kept up with the latest trends, but recognized some of the work by Belgian surrealists like Rene Magritte and Paul Delvaux. He'd never appreciated the sly visual puns of Magritte, but in the flesh, the works of Delvaux were quite intriguing. They were suffused with a dreamlike atmosphere; beautiful nudes wandered through dark, abandoned railway stations. They were certainly well executed, but Buchner decided a little cold for his taste. In fact, there was something quite eerie about them, in their moonlit stillness.

Buchner finished his drink. On the other side of the gallery a crowd dispersed and drifted towards him, whispering and smiling, as they returned to the bar. In their wake, on the far wall, hung the vast and corrupt flesh of it: Salvador Dali's painting *'The Face of War'*. It had travelled from town to city, crossed continents and oceans. It was here – the death's head burning in the fire at Veron's. The ungodly thing at the church of Ville-sur-Espérer. It was *here,* and Buchner felt all sensation drain from his body, the blood slow to a crawl in his veins.

The chatter and clamor of the casino faded to a muted crackle of white noise. A small, distant part of him pleaded to turn back, leave the casino, run through the streets...Buchner exhaled and took a step toward the painting. He moved sluggishly, like a sleepwalker trudging in a bad dream. He didn't know the sketch had been made into a finished work. He'd avoided reading anything about Dali. He dragged himself to the hate-stricken face, crushed into the gravity of its countenance.

Dali, in paranoiac-critical madness, had uncovered deeper truths as he set down its final form. The death's head was no longer a prison for writhing, tormented figures. It had become a hideous Russian doll, an endless succession of smaller skulls nesting in the cavities of its mouth and eye sockets, all the way down into a black, fractal infinity.

Buchner was transfixed, lost in the smooth, sepia flesh, the knotted shoal of carrion worms, the honeycombed hollows of its eyes. And slowly, the answers were revealed to him, neatly filed in the recesses of those mournful and infinite eyes. There was a limit to how many people could be locked into a church, before it was turned into a charnel house – say, a small village full. But here, there was a place for everyone: for Veron, for the little boy and girl, for the soldiers and civilians, for those who thought they'd survived the war.

Buchner stood before the painting, motionless, clutching his empty glass. He sensed people moving around him, muttering, laughing, taking a fleeting glimpse and returning to the gaming tables. It didn't matter. It made no difference if they could see it or not. Buchner had denied it for twelve years, though in his heart he'd known every brushstroke of that tattered, disembodied face. He slowly raised his right hand, and pressed it to the imprint of Dali's hand on the canvas. It fitted like a hand in glove. Buchner closed his eyes and nodded in silent assent.

He left the casino and walked into the street, drifting among the revelers, breathing in the cold air, the night and fog.

Lemmy Rushmore

This soldier...

it gnaws at my nerves
and it claws at my calm
this rifle now drenched
in the sweat of the palm

unspeakable acts
down the chain of command
your duty say they
and their weapon I stand

each life that I take
helps to take mine away
still here in this war
yet the mind ran astray

with one eye at watch
just pretending to sleep
in darkness I weep
as atrocities heap

the reason long lost
right along with my grip
but fight on I must
while on further I slip

eternally stained
by the rivers of blood
yet more I must let
seems I'll drown in the flood

though I'm rendered numb
I'm still loaded with pains
no longer what was
just this soldier remains...

Tom Nolan

If a Picture

My name is Johannes Mattheus Koelz. The album you see
before you contains fragments of my work, collected by
people unknown to me. These little pieces once belonged to
bigger pieces I destroyed in order to save something more
immediately precious. It was my intention to reconstitute
everything but that, like everything, is no longer within my
power.

The first part of me died in France in 1916. The rest of me
followed in 1971 – in Ireland, if I remember. That period of
my life was, as it is for many old people, vague. The earlier
years remain sharp.

I was a soldier in the First World Madness. My uniform
may not have been that of your ancestors but no matter. In
war – certainly in *that* war – men were game pieces,
moved about to settle the squabbles of maniacs who
dwelled safely in mansions and palaces. Had we been more
enlightened, organized or braver, both sides would have
joined forces to destroy our rulers. It would have been
interesting to see kings, presidents and chancellors hold a
rifle, cry for their mothers and shit themselves for their
obscene, useless lives.

(Perhaps I should have painted that?)

Like most of the young men who marched away from
childhood with heads swimming in dreams of glory, I felt
justified and proud. More, it embarrasses me to confess, I
felt privileged by the opportunity and I genuinely expected
to return in pride to a homeland that honored me for
protecting and enlarging its greatness. Death was like the
Yeti, time-travel or the peaceful coexistence of nations –
we thought it a possibility but we did not yet believe in it.

Soon we learned the reality of our mission was to turn countryside into mud and human beings into blood. Schlamm und Blut. Mud and blood. The words are contextually onomatopoeic in German, rhyming in English and operatic in paint. Of those who retained sufficient body parts to return home, many left their minds on the battlefield – another thing we had not considered.

At the time of which I need to speak, the war was going well for our side – for those of us who were still breathing. One afternoon we overran a Canadian position and found a sergeant on his knees praying for his life. It was Easter and some of the lads thought it would be amusingly seasonal to crucify him. In the absence of a cross and nails, they used bayonets and a stable door. A year previously, in their old lives, I believe they would all have been horrified by such an act. Six months ago they would not have done this thing. I had passed through the time when I might have risked putting the screaming man out of his misery. No one took his wedding ring.

These things were not uncommon on either side. In times of horror, men seek humour and it is rarely benevolent. I believe we were all sickened afterwards but when madness is all around, the only safe direction in which to look is away. You try to keep your body safe while steering your mind to a place where it hopes to be able to live with itself.

Unless you are an artist.

An artist must observe and document and portray and explain and somehow not become desensitized. He must march to the edge of self-destruction and look beyond. Titian told me recently that when he painted Actaeon torn apart for what he had observed, he was depicting himself. I think he rationalizes after the event but his point is true. If a painter loses his disgust, he cannot make others feel it, cannot persuade them never to take goodness for granted. Prattlers talk about suffering for their art. Usually this is a justification for earning no money but in war it is not a cliché. In war, the artist must compel himself to remain raw, to reject healing; he must pick continually at the scab. He does this by denying the easy condolences we feed to ourselves and to others. How easily and eagerly we coin, regurgitate and accept the reassurances:

"You poor thing, you had no choice/ You were just following orders/ Other people make the rules/ Your duty was to obey/ Your duty was to survive and to help your comrades survive/ What else could anyone do?"

The excuses used in war are especially dangerous because, whilst the things they seek to pardon are the most pernicious and ludicrous things of all, the reasons are often valid. The consequences of not obeying an order can be catastrophic for the individual and no less so for the intended victim. The order will be carried out by somebody. It is human nature to survive and no one is closer to nature than a soldier in a trench. The artist must succumb and strive to compensate for his weakness by remembering and re-feeling things any sane person would strive to forget. Otherwise nothing is gained.

Ghosts are useful for this. Ghosts metaphorical and actual serve to remind you. There were many ghosts in the trenches, waiting to welcome the next one, the next hundred, the next ten thousand to their ranks. We all saw them. We did not all admit this, even to ourselves.

On the night of the crucifixion, God appeared to me in my sleep. Whether it was a genuine holy or demonic visitation, an hallucination arising from mental and physical degradation or merely a dream, I still do not know. But this god knew me. He knew I wished never to forget, never to stop feeling what I had witnessed that day.

"So, Herr Koelz," he said, "you want to change the world? You have ideas above your station, my friend. Surely you know humans are granted only the illusion of that power. Is that not why you are all here, dying, maiming and killing each other for someone else's delusion?'

"I do not personally wish to change the world," I replied, "but to plant seeds that will grow to smother the weeds born of evil men's minds."

"So a painter is a farmer then?" *God* smiled and said, "You would think that I, being omniscient, would find questions redundant, wouldn't you?" He waited a moment but I did not get the joke so he laughed. "Just messing with you, boy. Without humor not even I could exist for all time and remain sane."

I think now that I suspected all was not as it seemed but I was prepared to ignore anything that did not suit my ambition. Such is the way of religion.

"I made you a painter, Johannes and I gave you a modicum of talent," *God* said.

"And I am grateful, Lord, but a modicum of talent is insufficient to record the events I wish to record in ways that might achieve the results I desire."

"That is true."

"Then my life is wasted."

"Like the lives of your fallen comrades, conceived in hope and destroyed in hubris?"

"Destroyed in vain," I heard myself say. "We rail against conflict with further aggression."

God smiled sadly and indicated the battlefield with a wave of his arm. "Mysterious ways beyond human understanding," he muttered along with something else I was unable to catch. Then he said it was his will to grant my wish.

"Then you will increase my ability?"

"Already done. Now I must get myself into a more official mood for the next bit; it's expected." *God* drew himself up. "Johannes Mattheus Koelz, henceforth you will possess the ability by means of the visual arts to portray the true essence of whatever you see. Thus may others understand that essence. Then perhaps, if they choose, they will influence destiny and improve the world. Who knows?"

"You?" I suggested.

God made a pistol of his index finger and thumb. "Yes sirree, Jo – but I'm not telling."

I squirm to admit that I then enquired if my art would make me famous. *God's* reply was that in all of history he had granted few people what he was giving me.

"And will I be rich?"

"If that is what you choose."

"Who would not choose to give their family a better life by doing what they love?"

The deity, demon or dream shrugged. "Decisions are not always conscious ones, Johannes. Your talent will open doors. Some doors you will not notice. Others you will decide not to walk through. There may even be some you barricade and run from. I will not influence you." He leaned toward me. "You have not asked if you will survive the war."

My heart convulsed. Was my success to be posthumous?

"You will live to be an old man. This war will end in two years."

And then he was gone. He gave me abilities beyond anything I could have imagined and he did not lie about my long life, but I think he was not God.

I tried a few tentative sketches during lulls in the fighting and found I could achieve effects beyond anything of which I had previously been capable. At first I did not trust or fully believe in this gift. Too often had I seen what war can do to a man's head, the delusions it begets. A combat soldier's view of reality is neither broad nor objective. Troops of all colours believe God is on their side or that He has forsaken them – never that He is either uninterested or disinterested in their personal fate. I was less naive.

Every day I less expected a shell to remove my head and, little by little, I began to believe in my destiny.

Two years later, the war ended. Officially, we had lost but I defy any sane person to claim anybody won.

In civilian life I became a policeman and rose through the ranks, always drawing, always painting, every spare moment. It was during this period I produced my triptych with the crucified soldier in the center panel.

Meanwhile, the National Socialist Party grew in strength, and disturbances of public order became frequent. I was tasked with putting down a Nazi riot and I carried out my duty efficiently and effectively. That, of course, did not stop them and we soon found ourselves in the Second World Madness. Clearly, twenty-one years was insufficient for my art to achieve its goal. Or was I not working hard enough?

So I painted in a Van Goghian frenzy and my reputation grew. I would have been arrested had the Gestapo seen some of my more revealing work but I was careful and kept the anti-heroic pieces to myself. Peacetime would be their time, a time they might help to prolong. I tried to stop producing those pieces, to store them in my head until they could safely be released. I owed it to my family to be cautious – and I believed I owed it to God to protect His gift. In my representational pieces, I strove to be superficial, little more than decorative, but I could not do it. For all my efforts, which did not at the time seem to be token ones, I had no restrictive control over my work. The ability to show the reality beneath the surface of things was in fact a *compulsion* to do so. Every day I lived in barely suppressed terror because the paintings I allowed people to see aroused admiration and comment, and in war governments have especially sharp ears.

These thoughts were running through my mind one morning as I gazed absently at my triptych, using it as a secular icon to focus my inner attention. There came a knock at the door. I threw a blanket over the triptych and scanned the studio for anything else that could be perceived as incriminating.

Another knock, louder, less patient. I opened the door with excuses ready to repel uninvited visitors but everything was forgotten as I gazed upon the smiling face of Adolph Hitler. It occurred to me this must be a look-alike, a prank organized by watching, giggling friends but the soldiers and armored vehicles in the road dispelled that notion.

"May I come in, Herr Koelz?"

"Of course, Mein Fuhrer." What else could I say – even if an alternative had presented itself to me?

The Austrian who ruled Germany stepped aside while two soldiers checked my studio for hidden assailants. Then they left and Hitler came in, closing the door behind him. He looked around and my heart sank even deeper as his eyes lingered on the covered easel. But he was a busy man and this was not a social call. "Herr Koelz, I will dispense with false modesty and presume you know me. Am I correct?"

"Of course, Mein Fuhrer."

He laughed. "Ah yes, you have already called me that. You will, I hope, also eschew a show of humility and agree with me when I say you are the greatest living German visual artist. I myself paint and I know talent when I see it." Again his eyes wandered around the room before returning to me and the business at hand. "There is no need to be nervous, Johannes – may I call you Johannes? Or do you prefer Matt?"

"Of course, Mein Fuhrer. Either."

He did not invite me to use the 'du' form or to call him by his first name but he put his arm around my shoulders. "If you are thinking of your pre-war activities against my party, please put those thoughts from your mind. You were doing your duty and I respect that." He laughed again. "It is a quality I rather demand of my subordinates."

I tried and failed to go with his humor and not be paralyzed by terror.

"Well, Johannes, time marches on, waiting for neither national leader nor international genius. So to business. I would be honored if you would permit me to commission a portrait of myself." He slapped my shoulder and withdrew his arm. "Good man. As for your fee, no doubt you would be timid in requesting what you deserve so I will decide, if that is all right with you. I promise to pay at least twenty times what you would have asked. Do we have a deal?"

Words were impossible so I merely nodded and tried to look deeply grateful for the opportunity.

"Excellent! Now if you will excuse me, I shall bid you good day. Someone will be in touch to arrange mutually convenient times for sittings."

And he was gone. A few moments later, engines roared into life and the motorcade moved off.

I fell back into a chair and squeezed the armrests. My God! A portrait of Hitler! Of course I couldn't do it – not because I could not do the sitter justice but because I couldn't *not* do that. Military national leaders are not people to whom one says 'no', however.

So I attempted a few oil sketches from photographs but instead of a Teutonic hero, out came – the Angel of Death, a slavering psychopath (a word I have since learned), a clown and, finally, a lost and pathetic human being. None of these would have been well received. My wife called it a dilemma but this was no difficult choice between two alternatives. I could paint *only* the truth. God had decreed it.

My only chance was to take my family and flee the country.

I could not abandon my triptych, my master work, but it was too cumbersome to carry and too large to conceal on a journey. So with a heavy heart, I photographed the panels and cut the pictures into six inch squares which I distributed amongst my friends. A few I kept. Some of these fragments in isolation displeased me so I destroyed them. Perhaps, I thought, this literal deconstruction should form a part of my future editing and re-drafting process.

Escape did not prove a simple matter. My family and I had many frights and adventures I will not go into here. On two occasions, I knew fear on a par with the worst I had experienced during the First World Madness – greater fear, because I was afraid for my loved ones. If this were a film, those events would be the *poster moments*. For me, it is sufficient they are over. But of course you know all this already. You are conversant with my flight from Germany to England, where I was interned as an enemy alien, and my subsequent descent into old age in Ireland.

Possibly you think me immodest in assuming you know me but we must be realistic and time is short. One thing Adolph Hitler was right about was his low opinion of false humility. It wastes time and achieves nothing. Great art, like dead fish, will always rise to the surface, so forgive me if I mention myself in the same breath as Rembrandt, Leonardo and Picasso. In my lifetime I was more successful than Van Gogh but the fame I was promised had in large part to be posthumous. That is acceptable because, like Van Gogh, I ...

But your face is etched in uncomprehending lines as you look from me to the album and then in embarrassment to the floor. You are clearly no philistine yet you know neither the name nor the work of Johannes Mattheus Koelz. How embarrassing for us both.

Please allow me a moment to compose myself.

I apologize for wasting your time and my own. Has anyone ever acted differently because of a picture? Certainly not the right people. Those who need to change do not look at art. Hitler would have looked, but would he have seen? Sufficiently to make him disappointed and angry but probably no more.

And what of you? Assuming I *could* influence you, to what extent does it lie within your power to change the world? To what degree is it consistent with your desire? Probably now I will never know. All I can do is leave you my triptych, created, dismantled, reassembled and preserved by people unknown to history. We live, we love, we fight, we die. Nothing changes except through the actions of the anonymous many. Only the names of those who send others to their deaths are remembered by the living.

And yet the artist in all of us must persevere and record and hope.

Raymond Walker

and blast them all

Albert Tutte, war hero, brought glory

Damn them! Damn
and blast them all!

Deep breath.   Control yourself.

I'll start again. No more outbursts. I must respect
convention. Tonight, I'm the storyteller. Tonight, I stoke
the fire that keeps the wolves at bay.
   Back to Albert Tutte then.
   Our hamlet surrendered seven of its sons to the cause.
Rushed them away at the tail end of harvest. The war had
already been raging for two months. Chances for glory on
the battlefield might end at any moment.
   See the squat, rust-colored train station? See our motley
band on the boardwalk? They're playing Song of the Allies.
"I sing a song of Britain, I can tell of her might . . ." A
catchy tune, don't you think? Oh well, they're not
professional musicians. You see Alice? The frizzy-haired
one in the middle? Portly, flustered? Warbling loudly and
off key? She's our music teacher. The red-faced, little man
in the gray coveralls muttering to himself? Rudy, our
reluctant mayor. He manages the grain elevator. What
does he know about speechifying? You can spot the fathers.
Faces beaming, chests out-thrust. The weeping mothers
console each other. Our heroes! Round cheeked, barely
shaving. Look at their self-conscious grins. They're so
young! First time away from home. Let's name them
because they will be in the spotlight for such a short time:

56

They are (from left) little Randy Beaton, the big Swedes
Ollie and Carl Anderberg, Albert, Wilber Watts (eldest of
nine brothers, biting at his cheek), and the bully Harold
Rasmussen (scowling as always). The laughing one with
the tight black curls? That's Billy Tetachuck.

One son the hamlet reluctantly
kept
for itself.
The gargoyle with the
contorted
body
who should've died at
birth, the spastic,
not fit   for war.
Not fit for   anything.

Deep breath. Deep breath.
Panicking
makes it worse. Makes it harder to
think. Remember to
breathe.

Breathe.

The Almighty, in His infinite wisdom, created the
deformed wretch so people would remember to be thankful
for their own good fortune and bless the Creator for their
own perfectly formed limbs. That's what a scolding mother
told her gawking children one sunny morning as they
passed by on the street. People often presume him deaf. Or
incapable of feeling. People, for some reason, often cite a
vengeful creator when they seem him.
   His mother calls him Lawrence. Children call him snotty.
He prefers Larry.
   Oh yes, the boys. I get sidetracked so easily.

Randy was killed in a plane crash while training in England. Word of Harold's death came in a terse notice a few months later. "The report is to the effect that he was killed in action." Ollie, Carl, and Wilber died at Passchendaele. News of Billy's death came in September, only days before Albert's return.

They all died heroes. It was the meagre scrap to which grieving parents clung. They sacrificed their lives in a noble campaign against an evil empire. Newspapers clamored about German atrocities - babies bayonetted, civilians' eyes gouged, rape, mutilation, children given hand grenades to play with.

"I don't think we can always trust what we read," Larry's mother warned one night after his father cursed and threw down the evening paper including the story about a Canadian soldier crucified with bayonets to a barn door. She waited until she was alone with her son, though.

She was not so politic the day she learned of Billy's death. "What need have we of another dead hero!" she exclaimed.

Larry's father glared. "Damn it, woman," he said and stomped off to get the tin tub for bath night. She put her head next to her son's. Her cheek moist. He loved the weight of his mother's head on his bony shoulder.

Mother. Nurse. Transportation. Entertainment. Translator. She was everything to him. He couldn't manage something as simple as holding a newspaper. He couldn't talk. People certainly didn't talk to him. He watched and listened. He was good at that.

"But that's all you have to do," she said. "If you know your neighbours, you know the world."

Albert was the weakest and the clumsiest of the boys who went away. His little sister Beth, the ruddy-cheeked, big-boned farm girl Larry thought almost as beautiful as his mother, was more help with chores than her brother. But it was Albert who came home with a medal, a bronze bauble dangling from a crimson ribbon. A crowned lion atop another crown with the words Pro Valore underneath. He showed it to everyone. Well, almost everyone. Larry managed a glimpse when Albert knelt for toothless old Mrs. Watson.

I get ahead of myself.
The clock - tick, tick, tick - unnerves me.
So hard to keep things in order.

Where were we? Oh, yes. Saying goodbye. There's the band, again. Now they're playing 'Till the Boys Come Home.' *"They were summoned from the hillside/They were called from the glen . . ."* Alice, always out of tune, doesn't even notice, or maybe just ignores, the glares of her fellow choir members. Look at the crowd there on the platform. Larry is easy to pick out. He's the man-child with the cotton diapers puffing out his pants. Beside him a slender woman stands defiantly, shoulders back, chin out. Only Larry, feeling the trembling of her hand on his shoulder, knows how nervous she is.

His mother.

She is a bit disheveled. Her hair is parted off centre and escapes in delicate wisps from her low, loose bun. Oh, but her delicate skin! Those high cheekbones! She has bags under her eyes, but they are beautiful eyes, wide set and bluer than the ribbon on Beth's bonnet. It can't be easy being Larry's mother. He's getting weaker. He sees the anxiousness in her face at night. Pooling mucus cuts off his breath and he wakes gagging. She's always there, cool hand stroking his forehead. She's ferocious in her love. It's her strength that has kept him alive so long.

The glowering man with arms folded over his thick chest at the other end of the platform? Larry's father. He won't stand near his son. He yearns for Larry's death. He's wanted it from the moment he saw him mewing like a misshapen toad at his mother's breast.

Larry doesn't hate his father.

That's not true.
He hates
him.
He tries not
to.

He can understand his dad's disappointment. What good is a crooked-spined son who will never be able to throw a bale, drive a tractor, or caress a woman's body? Okay, maybe the woman's body was more the son's regret. He often tried to imagine what Beth would look like without clothes.

The only naked woman he has ever
seen is his mom.
His father, too much in the
drink, forced himself upon her,
refused her entreaties to turn
Larry's wheelchair away.

It is
hard
to
talk about
this.
Breathe.   Breathe.

His mother is pensive beside Larry. She knows she's not welcome. She has been ostracized since her suggestion over sandwiches at the end of the Rebekah's meeting that perhaps they could discuss their support of the war. The only one who will talk to her is Billy, even though his father frowns. Billy even says goodbye to Larry. Gives him a friendly slap on the shoulder. She knows, just as well as she knows the coming winter will bring frigid winds and drifting snow, that war will not be as easy as they claim and that some of these boys won't return. She hangs on to Billy's hand.

She was right, of course.

Randy's body came home.

The 'We regret to inform you' letter arrived for Ollie's and Carl's parents.

"Who knew?" the townsfolk bleated. "They said it would end quickly! They said they would come home. They said they would come home." They whined. How they whined.

Bleated. Whined.
I can't conceal my contempt.
I can't forgive them.

"They should have known. They were the adults. They were children. The parents should have known." That's what Larry's mom said, the night she learned of Billy's death. "Damn and blast them all!" Her son blinked. She never swore.

She had watched those boys grow up.

She babysat little Billy for eleven months when his mother, a sickly woman who barely survived her first pregnancy, died during her second attempt and her husband went back to England to find a new wife. Billy sat in her kitchen eating oatmeal cookies while she patted Larry's back to loosen the phlegm in his lungs. He even helped sometimes. Larry remembers that patting; so tentative it made his mother laugh.

Billy
was
afraid to
hurt him.

"It's not okay to be ignorant when you send your children off to be slaughtered," said his mother as she lathered his skinny body, careful of the raw spots on his buttocks. Larry twitched his agreement, (occasionally his body responds to his commands) and the grey bathwater (mom first, then dad, then Larry) slopped over the sides of the tub onto the checkered kitchen linoleum.

"Even if the war were over, even if our boys had killed the Germans, probably boys like themselves, and come home to us, how could we think they wouldn't be damaged by the violence? How stupid we are! Like bleating sheep. Baa, baa, baa!" He couldn't have argued with her reasoning even if he had been capable. He might, however, have asked her to be less vigorous with the scrub brush.

"There are so many villains in this war," she said later when he was in bed and she was about to begin reading to him. Tonight it was Dorian Gray. Every night she read to him. She taught him to read too, even some French and Italian. Not to speak, of course. He was equally inarticulate in all languages. She was not comfortable with math and it became his weakness too. He was oversupplied with weaknesses. Bedtime stories kept away the night terrors. Gave him something to think about when joint pains kept him awake. "Stories, like a bonfire on a frosty night, keep at bay the ferocious animals lurking in our consciousness." They both laughed when she read that. Larry's father snorted and noisily rustled his newspaper. He rarely approved of her choice of reading material.

Her mind was not on literature this night though.

"I hate the chest-thumping politicians, the incompetent, bloodthirsty generals, the war profiteers who grow rich from the misery of others." Larry sputtered and jerked his arms, like he was clapping with his elbows. Hate was a word she never used. "But I'm afraid the greatest blame must fall on these grieving mothers and fathers, these good folk who tend their fields, quote scripture and exchange pleasantries over their backyard fences." She mistook his grunting and thrashing for agreement. He just wanted her to begin reading. "Of all the villainy, of all the treachery in this enduring war, none is as great as this easy betrayal of our children." The sadness in her voice clutched at his heart and made him regret his selfishness.

When they forayed on their daily errands Larry berated his neighbours. Nincompoops, he said, spluttering. Complacent, self-indulgent cowards! He jerked so spasmodically in his chair his mother had to lay a restraining hand on his shoulder. Hypocrites! Pharisees! Righteous, spiteful, puffed-up Christians! He mocked them for their blind conformity, their willful ignorance, the intellectual laziness that let them assuage the guilt they felt for the death of their sons by bullying the one person who had the courage from the beginning to say the war was a mistake. And though he knew as soon as he spoke that it was cruel; that he was stooping to their level, he told them it was their fault their boys had died alone and so far from home! They were to blame. Those deaths were a judgment.

How simple he was. If only he had known. Those deaths on the battlefield were just the beginning. Scattered rain drops before the deluge.

"We have to understand," said his mother, whispering in his ear. "They have lost children in this conflict. It is more important than ever for them to believe, otherwise they will have to admit their sons died for nothing."

Larry could not be so charitable. He laughed. He spat.

There! You see them at Roland Elves' grocery story in the aisle between the pork and beans and the Quaker Oats. There's Mrs. Moran with her daughter visiting from the city. The younger Moran is wearing a short skirt. She probably thinks Larry is staring lasciviously at her slim ankles in those tight, lace-up boots, which he is. See how they glare, see how their lips tighten, how they look away and whisper? Of course they don't understand him. They don't know they are being insulted. His face is always contorted.

> He is always gurgling,
> always drooling.
> Would he have spoken out if there
> wasn't this unbridgeable disconnect of
> mind and body?
> If people could actually
> understand?
> He doesn't think he
> would be so brave as his mother.

In his mind, his words are perfectly formed. They issue eloquently from gracefully pursed lips and his gestures are grand and fluid. He would make such speeches! The mayor would be shamed to silence. Prime ministers and presidents would come to hear him speak. He would not lie about heroic deaths and noble sacrifices. Lesser men could sing the glories of war. Obfuscating politicians, reluctant to offend, could pacify the placid masses with pretty phrases, easy patriotism and clichés. He would not be so disingenuous. He would thunder at the audience. He would be as remorseless and vengeful as the Old Testament God who called forth a deluge to rid the world of sinners. He would berate the throngs for their stupidity. For their cowardice. Their selfishness. Their stunted imaginations. Their greed. Their lust and wonton fornications. (Okay, maybe not the lust and wanton fornications. He had himself certainly lusted and if the opportunity had been there he was reasonably sure he would have also have wantonly fornicated.)

"If you could speak, what wise things you would say," his mother often told him. If only she knew. What wise and terrible things he would say. They would not be able to turn away. People would know the truth of his words and would weep to hear their weakness laid bare before them.

Lost my train of thought.
Coughing fit.
Spittle cools on my chin.
Where am I? Oh, yes.
Albert comes home.

Farm boys went away. A hero returned. Meadowlarks sang. The setting sun turned the stubble gold in Beaton's field. There's Larry and his mom again at the train station, still apart from the others. Arched back, protruding jaw, perpetual grimace exposing decaying teeth. He is repulsive. Monstrously so. He doesn't blame children for staring or girls for turning away, but he scorns them for assuming an ugly person can't appreciate beauty. And what is there
in the wide
world to rival the
magnificence
of a prairie
sunset on a mild
fall evening?
The welcome back was a muted affair. No band this time. No banner. No speeches. How do you celebrate one man's return, when so many didn't? The Anderbergs weren't there. They grieved in their darkened living room. People applauded when Albert, pale and unsmiling, stepped off the train. His mom and dad embraced him. He was impressive in his green rifle regiment's tunic with the slanted cuff, the detachable shoulder boards and the nine glittering buttons down the front. After four years at war he was still scrawny. The pimples were gone though. The Anglican Minister said a prayer and the assembly dispersed.
Albert had one day at home.

See his parents? How proud they are? They clutch his arms like they can't believe he has returned. They march him house to house, still in his uniform. They steer him to the other side of the street when they see Larry and his mom. The mayor, drunk before lunch, is the lesser of two evils.

"So what was it like over there?" the mayor asks loudly. Albert merely shrugs.

That night, Albert had no appetite for roast beef and potatoes. A cold, they thought. Stuffy nose. Coughing. Sneezing. His muscles and joints ached. Sore throat. A fever that became dangerously high. All within a few hours.

Hard to be calm.
I bang my head against
the leather padding
at the back of my chair.
I weep. Snot
clogs my throat.
I know what
lies ahead.

The nearest doctor was ten miles away. He was too much occupied to help. He sent word of a ferocious pestilence. Stay inside. Avoid contagion, he warned. Albert was dead before noon the next day.

He died gasping for
air,
face blue, bloody
froth
on his lips.

His parents and Beth, who, in Larry's fantasies, adored his supple fingers and dry wit, also died. Billy's new mother and little sister were the next to go.

Tick, tick tick. Dogs
bark. Beaton's cows, impatient
to be milked, low
incessantly.
Coyotes yap, brazen now
there is no one guarding the
chickens.
Too dark to
see in the
house.
I imagine her staring
at me.
Reproachingly.
My heart, a lump of
congealed
porridge, insists on beating.
If they don't
find me dead
when they finally
come,
they will   find me   mad.
Breathe!   Breathe!

People locked themselves away. They wore masks when
they had to go outside. Never was there such a need for the
comfort of communal prayer, but both churches were
empty on Sundays. Even the priests stayed home. The
general store closed when Roland died. His widow would
not leave the house. It was retribution. End of days.

Larry's mom would not stay home though she had to defy
her husband. It was the only time in Larry's life he ever
sided with his father.

"Somebody has to help," she said simply.

"Your stubbornness will be your death," said Larry's dad, who subsequently removed himself to the hired-hand's vacant shack on the outskirts of town.

"It's hard not to see this as a punishment," she said that first night. She had been at the Hopkin's house where father and son were stricken. The dad lived. The five-year-old, a stout blond-haired boy who only the day before had been playing hopscotch with his sisters, died like the rest, drowning in his body fluids.

Sometimes she would not come home until late in the night. She nursed the Tuttes and the mayor and all those others who had shunned her for speaking out against the war, who had gossiped about what wickedness on her part had brought about the divine retribution of a freakish first born. Mrs Anderberg, still mourning Ollie and Carl, begged her forgiveness. She died within minutes of her husband. Their remaining two sons also died. The only ones who survived in that doomed house were a baby girl and the sickly grandmother.

"Who are we to judge?" Larry's mom said, kissing Larry's cheek through the cotton mask covering her face. Her voice was so weak he could barely hear. "I wonder if they are no more responsible for their prejudices than I am for my small kindnesses. Who decides how we live? And how we die? I feel a randomness to this scourge. An indifference that scares me more than mere death."

She knelt beside Larry and prayed. She was so weary she had to hold on to his wheelchair. Larry grunted his amusement. He had no faith in a god that created him as a lesson for others. But that wasn't the funny part. The priest praised his god for bringing Albert home alive. But if the priest praised him for that, he must also blame him for this influenza,
    this relentlessly
    chirping bird Albert
    brought home in his pocket.

He wondered that his mother did not see the irony. But even he, the atheist, was chilled by the despair in her words.

The healthiest suffered the most. That was the odd thing. Old Mrs Watson, who kissed Albert's cheek and stroked his medal, only got the sniffles. The infirm, like Larry, vulnerable to the mildest of colds, never got sick at all. A few got the illness and survived. The fever just went away.

Larry's mother found her husband feverish in bed a week after he sequestered himself in the shack. He scorned sickness, but that day was too weak to stand. He was a strong man so, following the influenza's strange logic, he succumbed quickly. Woozy at breakfast. Dead at lunch. An early death for the father who wished an early death for the son.

She wept.

Larry didn't.

That night he woke up choking. His mother appeared as usual in his doorway, but came no closer. Stood impassively. Why was she not helping? She changed into the mayor, hiding a whisky bottle behind his back. "I feel a randomness to this scourge. An indifference that scares me more than mere death," he said, staggering, not from drunkenness, but from sickness. Larry cried out: "I am glad for your infection. I am glad for your death!" Then he woke, gagging. Choking in earnest this time. Later, limp between rumpled sheets, he worried over his mother's absence.

She came finally. Her face chalk-white. She struggled to get him dressed. It was almost too much for her to get him into the wheelchair. She lay on the couch to rest a moment before getting breakfast.

"I am just so tired. I have never been this tired."

She never got up again.

Her throat was sore.

She ached all over.
She called
for water.

She called her husband in a voice Larry didn't recognize.
She called for her mother and father. Her sister, long dead.
She even called for Larry. She must have been delirious.
What could he do? He flapped his arms. He squirmed. He
croaked. "Ungh, ungh, ungh." Even if somebody had been
standing at the door they would not have heard. Her face
was shiny with sweat.

How can I
continue? What kind of
bedtime story is this?
A comedy would have been
more appropriate.
I don't want to
breathe.

The midday sun was warm on Larry's neck when she lay
down. He was in the shadows when she died. The evening
light slanted through the stained-glass window in the living
room and illuminated with a saintly glow the couch where
she struggled. She wanted water. It was not fair that she,
who was there for everybody else, should die unattended.
Foolish naivety to expect fairness! Purple welts on her
arms,
neck. Torture to
hear her gasping. He
groaned. Rocked.
Closed his eyes. Couldn't
stop his ears. Wished
his own death. Wished his
persistent heart,   beating violently
in his deformed chest,

would disintegrate.

Breathe.　　　Breathe.

Blood-tinged
froth.
Blood
dribbling.
From her
ears.
Her nose.

Breathe!　　Breathe!

It is monstrously unjust that I, so close to death for so
long, live while others, so much in health, have expired! I
cling stubbornly, stupidly, to the absurd notion of fairness!
Have I not learned?
　The fire has dwindled. Only embers now. Wolves creep. I
feel their hot breath on my neck. Time for another story. It
is my turn. She has told me so many over the years.

Albert Tutte, war hero, brought glory to our hamlet . . .

Eve Gaal

Wife on the Front/PTSD

I married the four-year-old
who can't get past the impassable.
Papers please?
Stuck
at the border crossing from hell.
Gruff and unsure-
Unwilling to admit fear,
on a soapbox.
Ready to pounce
Or protect.
World weary,
Lugging repetitive war stories,
Open unstitched scars-
Wounds his mother never saw--
That never healed.
A wolf without a pack
A lion without a pride
Lost on the savannah
Licking raw pain
Growling at his cubs-
Alone in a crowd.

Am I ready for the task?
If I remove a single thorn
Will the others grow back?
He pledged loyalty
But will it endure?
Must I empathize or sympathize
Or just be wise?
Can I bear his cross of war?

The agony of rationed terror,
The mindless evils of revolutions
The dust rubble in his mind?

Do wedding vows see beyond boots
Goose-stepping into our lives?
Will they remind me of my own sorrows,
My own superficial wounds?
Which tickle with too much sun--
Like tangy lemonade--
brings tears to my eyes.
I lose touch with my own pain
For that, I'm grateful.
It's an honor just trying to understand,
His heart--
or that stoic face--
A vision of pride
When the flag unfurls.

Let him howl.
Let him roar.
I am the only one left
and yes,
I will kiss all his boo-boos.

Roger Cowin

Men at War

We are crossing the wash.
The scent of mayhem
hangs heavy in the thick air.
A virus of violence infects us.
There is no reason for it.
We are young and don't believe in death.
not our own leastways.
We can imagine ourselves
The Bringers of Death
but never the victims.
We are invincible.

No one dares break this uneasy silence.
Only the flickering ash-glow of cigarettes
and the funeral hum of insects
disturbs the solemn parade.
There is no reason for it.
We dream of home,
we dream of backyard barbecues
and baseball games on the radio,
sipping cold beers on a lazy, Sunday afternoon.
We dream of life,
we dream of sweethearts and wives,
the breasts of young women
pressed against our bare skin,
hasty couplings in the backseat of old Chevys.
We dream, we dream.
Dreams extinguished in the sharp retort
of sudden sniper fire,
bullets striking against helmet.

There is no reason for it.
We drop where we stand,
some down into the shallow water,
others onto the forest floor.
Shouting our battle cries,
we return fire,
become one beast,
a primal force, bringing death
with animal fury.

CS Nelson

SNAP TCP!

(H-8)

The announcer's voice booms with professional clarity. "Ladies and gentlemen." A hardly decorated officer with a mic. "The ceremony will begin in two minutes." The commissioned asshole reminds everyone to, "Please take this time to silence all electronic devices." Stupid dick lieutenant just can't get enough. "Thank you."

"You're not welcome." Spence says it through clenched teeth. He hates military ceremony, and the Army seems to have one for every gaddamned day.

"This shit's retarded," Specialist Jason Bortoff says *not* under his breath but out loud. Real loud. Loud like he always says everything loud. The thing about Bortoff, the guy's kinda whack, but at the same time he is so gaddamned *real*. SPC Maximillian Spence cuts his eyes right to left, making sure their platoon sergeant didn't hear. One more hour, then the Thunder Troop Unit Organizational Day starts with some mean flag football and ends in Spence's Thunderpalooza barracks party.

If Bortoff can just keep his gaddamned cool long enough. Spence relaxes. No one heard. They're good so far.

"Dude," Spence says. "Chill."

Bortoff rolls his eyes and holds his middle finger in a straight up salute between them. Spence settles. Bortoff has everything under control, just like always, just like months ago in Mosul, Iraq. The announcer lieutenant dick leans into the mic at the front of the stage. Spence nods along. This is going to be one helluva killer night.

"Ladies and gentlemen, please stand for the entry of the

Official Party and remain standing for the playing of the national anthem and the benediction."

A regal march *bhomp-bhomp-bhomps* from the US Army Signal Corps amplifier. Lieutenant Colonel Hanover, a lanky African American, steps to his own time despite the cadence blatting from the speakers. Beside him, Command Sergeant Major Lynch, a slightly shorter Irish bulldog, keeps pace until they stand in front of their seats directly beneath the podium.

The music stops. A drum roll ushers forth from the video clip of tanks, artillery, and squads of infantrymen, all blasting away to a distorted MP3 of the national anthem. It ends. Silence spreads across the crowd. A chaplain in his Army combat uniform steps up to the podium.

"Let us pray." He does so for everyone, and it takes forfuckingever. "Amen."

LTC Hanover thanks the chaplain and speaks into the mic, his voice reminiscent of James Earl Jones, but with some hella severe southern accent. "Mothers and fathers," he says. "Sons and wives," he continues. "We thank you all for coming to this our finest day of victory and homecoming."

The next ten minutes are sacrificial ones Specialists Bortoff and Spence will never get back, LTC H up there talking words-words-words. But CSM Lynch's introduction of their special guest makes it all worth the ass pain.

"Not everyone makes it home," Sergeant Major says. "But we are blessed to have with us today a young man we should all admire." CSM Lynch pulls the mic from the stand to wade into the audience. He likes to do that. Spencer's seen him do it a million times. It's how the sawed-off Sergeant Major always catches Joes sleeping during his stupid fucking briefs.

But this time it's priceless.

The mic gets stuck in the holder.

He yanks. The podium rocks. Dumbass Opie Taylor-looking Master Sergeant Simmons jumps up to help him, and they both manage to knock the podium on its ass. Bortoff laughs uber loud and fake. Spence ribs Bort, and it gets all quiet and nervous again, but now with his best friend giving him stink-eye.

CSM Lynch says something through a toothy grin more predator than friend. MSG Simmons nods and moves off stage, returning shortly with a couple of Staff pukes in tow to fix their shit. CSM Lynch turns back to the quiet-nervous-smiling-uncomfortable crowd.

"Like I need a damned mic anyway," he says.

Twitchy laughter rolls through the front row, picking up momentum toward the third, petering out to a bored sigh by the fifth. True to his word, CSM Lynch bellows in his command voice without needing an amp. "Within the first three months of our deployment, we dropped from 172 significant acts of violence per week against coalition forces to a mere seventeen. IEDs. Car bombs. Small arms attacks. RPG ambushes. We locked those sons of bitches down taut, and then drove them back to the very fires of hell where the cowards belong."

"IEDs," Spence says in a soft drone, like a Wikipedia entry. "Improvised Explosive Devices."

Bortoff shakes his head, perturbed. "Dude, don't start that shit again."

Spence rolls his fingertips against his thumbs, his hands fidgety beetles in contrast to his dull eyes and slow breath. He continues, voice a steady monotone, a touch of Asperger's driving his left brain. "Formed from commonplace and industrial items at hand. Coffee cans, empty propane tanks, sewage pipes, etcetera. The bomb maker fills the vessel with explosives and packs it full of anything skin-ripping. Screws, bolts, rivets, razors or just cut triangles and shavings from some auto shop in town. Then he blows it up when a US troop gets near. Walla. Insta-mess."

Bortoff gives in to Spence's eerie spell. "Fuckers."

CSM Lynch continues, "But the streets were far from safe. It was during a routine patrol. One of our finest platoons followed their instincts and the recommendation of their linguist and exceptional patriot, Mr. Ibrahim "Mike" Naji, and set up a hasty traffic control point in an effort to intercept the biggest insurgent financier in operation." He scans the audience, then adds, "And that Snap TCP was a valorous success, ladies and gentlemen. A sorely won victory costing us an excellent specimen of a sergeant and robbing another outstanding warrior of his dream to win the Seattle Marathon."

The crowd swells with a morbid cloud of regret. Everybody knows who Sergeant Major's talking about.

CSM Lynch pushes the story. "The young soldier and his NCO manned the checkpoint from behind their Humvee at H-hour, while their driver and gunner pulled long-range security for Escalation of Force protocol."

"EOF," Spence says, again barely a murmuring of how-to steps in time to his piano fingers. "Escalation of Force. Three hundred meters we hold a sign that says, 'Slow the fuck down,' in Arabic. Two hundred meters we string concertina wire and drop big flashing markers. One hundred meters out we have a no-shit Arabic STOP sign. After that, we start shooting. Every Haji on the gaddamned planet knows this."

Spence drove that day. Bortoff was on the gun, an M2 "Ma Deuce" .50 caliber machine gun with enough punch to blow through a Chevy big block.

"The car in question, identified by the young soldier from the daily BOLO list," CSM Lynch says, his voice quiet but reverberating in the stillness of the auditorium, "pulled up to the checkpoint. Mr. Naji, the linguist, recognized the vehicle and approached the car as it came to a halt at the platoon's Snap TCP barrier."

"Fucking terp," Bortoff says under his breath.

Spence crushes his active fingertips in his fists. He feels it, too. The anger. The loss. "Gaddamn Mike."

"PFC Jonathan Wheeler noticed something was not right and placed himself between the unarmed linguist and the suspect. The driver held up his cell phone without looking at it—"

—Spence's fists flower into hammering fingers—

"— and began to pray to Allah feverishly," CSM Lynch says.

"Cell phone detonators," Spence mumbles. "Cheap. Throwaways. Always unmarked. The average electrical output of a cell ringer is less than 3 volts, but when used in conjunction with a detonator being drip fed voltage just below trigger threshold, the tiniest spark will set off the chain reaction needed to create ignition."

Bortoff doesn't say a word, but his nose curls into a silent snarl.

"At H-hour and a handful of seconds into the platoon's Snap TCP, the driver panicked and detonated his vehicle-borne IED even as PFC Wheeler threw himself at the linguist and saved them both."

The Sergeant Major milks the silence for effect. Spence keeps his eyes straight ahead like everyone else.

"But I am proud to stand here today and tell you our warriors are made of unbreakable steel. An incredible young man missed his dream of winning the Seattle Marathon by one day last year because he deployed early, an unstoppable machine embodying the heart of every Thunder Troop warrior," CSM Lynch's voice rises to a preacher's crescendo. "And though the enemy may have robbed him of his gold medal legs, it has only stoked the fire in his heart. Let's hear it for newly promoted SPC Jonathan Wheeler who *will* bring home the *gold* next week at the Seattle Marathon's *Wheelchair* Division."

Thunderous applause swells, and people pop up for an ovation, first in prairie dog onsies-twosies, then as a herd.

Beside Spence, Bortoff's breath fires out his nostrils. Hot, angry clouds of hate. The kind of breathing Spence heard in his headset that day just before Bortoff squeezed off burst after uncontrolled burst at the surrounding civilians and buildings. No one was harmed, but plenty of gaddamned damage was done.

The Sergeant Major finishes on a high. "SPC Wheeler, come up here and join us, son."

Everyone's standing and pounding their dickbeaters together. Bortoff, too, only the grin on his face seems focused. Dialed in. "Oh yeah, Wheels. Tonight's yours."

Spence smiles. It *is* going to be a good night.

"Gaddamned right, Bort."

Bortoff pats him on the shoulder, confiding. Trusting. Battle Buddies forever.

(H-6)

"Daddy!" Nadiyah's sixteen-year-old voice rages, "It's not fair!" Then a calmer, "Besides, I promised Jeffrey I'd use my ID Card to get us on post."

Ibrahim Naji breathes deeply through his nostrils and pleads with tired eyes to the ceiling.

"Nadiyah. This is not about fairness. It is about what is right. You are a young woman and should not mingle with certain crowds." But his voice sounds stale even to his ears. "You are forbidden to attend this soldiers' beer party!"

His wife, Saraih, clears her throat. "Nadiyah, it is important for a beautiful Arabic woman to maintain her reputation," she says, her hands clasped primly in front of her elegant-print thawb and hijab long-scarf.

"Mother." Nadiyah's eyes smolder with indignation. "What of my reputation?"

"Enough," Ibrahim says. He is no longer interested in arguing. "You will not go with this Jeffrey, and that is final."

Nadiyah continues to tear him apart with her eyes.

"Besides, he is not right in the mind. We all know this to be true—"

"Why?" she cries. "Because he loves me, Daddy? Because he wants to embrace our culture? Is that why you hate him?"

Saraih soothes their daughter. "Nadiyah, he is a confused young man and, while he may wish to support you, claiming Islam and changing names to prove one's heart is not necessarily the way to go about it. Give him time to mature—"

"But he *loves* me, Mother!"

"He's an idiot!" Ibrahim stands and meets his daughter's baleful gaze, waits for the inevitable crumbling-to-tears, and turns away to give her time to bury herself sobbing into Saraih's bosom.

Neither Saraih nor their daughter truly understands the seriousness of the crowd with which Nadiyah's boyfriend associates himself. And for all that is holy, Ibrahim cannot fathom why. How could a man still yet a child decide to up and change his religion? And to such extremes! *Muhammed Al Ghandi?* Rubbish. The boy's chosen naming convention is the equivalent of a cartoon. And what could possess a seventeen-year-old American boy to want so desperately to rub shoulders with the same platoon Ibrahim himself had served?

"Not all soldiers are good, Nadiyah," he says, his voice drowned beneath her childlike sobs.

(H-4)

D-Day. The first Higgins boat lands at Normandy, and Tom Hanks rallies his men. The new Skrillex/Korn mix drops to all time subterranean lows. Walls shake beneath Spence's pulverizing Bose subs. The boat's ramp drops, and bullets slaughter panic-stricken seasick troops.

Horrifying casualties, strobing death in the black light.

"Drink, fuckers!" Bortoff bellows with the command of a drill sergeant.

Bottles and glasses rise to sloppy lips, toasting the plasma TV on the wall, the world in black, white, and sepia-tone annihilation. Small quarters meant to hold two to four men, is packed with twelve bristling, belching, farting, over-sexed male beasts. Infantry soldiers fresh from deployment.

"Wait," Wheels slurs, leaning against the side of his wheelchair. "Why'd we drink, again?" The TV splash mixed with the club lighting turns his face into a little kid.

Bortoff throws an arm across Wheels's shoulders and explains, "It's the rules, dude. We watch a show, and every time someone gets shot? We drink. See?"

"The actual D-Day casualties at the Omaha Beach sector," Spence says, "is an historically excepted guess of about 2000, not counting airborne."

"Ohh—"

On the television, a German pillbox .30 cal machine gun rips through the first wave of Doughboys piling into the beachhead.

"Drink!"

Someone pounds on the door. It opens, and a hand pops up wielding a bottle of Jack Daniels above the sweat-and-liqueur miasma.

Spence can't feel his face, and Bortoff is rock steady as always. Spence nods too much and grins at his battle buddy. Bortoff's eyes crinkle into the same smile Spence remembers from deployment. His best friend. *Always there for me?* He asked it through tears after Wheels got hit at the TCP. *Yeah, bud. Always.* Bortoff held Wheels like he really cared that day. Loved, even. *And we're gonna make this right. Promise.*

And here they are with Wheels in the middle. Again. Making it right.

Another rapid-fire tattoo of fists beat at the door.

"Girl on deck," Someone yells. The TV volume drops.

"Yo! At-ease, make way," another says.

Spence squints through the crowd. It *is* a female.

And a gadddamned Iraqi one.

"Oh, bring it, baby," Bortoff says, a devilish leer splitting his face. "About to get HME all up in here."

"HME," Spence recites, fingers rolling slowly across his thumbs. "Homemade Explosives. Formed by breaking up a 33.4%- 35% nitrogen-concentrated ammonium nitrate fertilizer—that's right, dicks, *fertilizer*—with powder-form fuels. Like sugar. Like cinnamon. If it's rust colored and smells like your great gram's snickerdoodle cookies, the shit's lethal. HME is extremely unstable, and bomb makers are often identified in public by missing fingers, usually from their left hands as Islamic custom dictates the right hand is sacred."

"Assholes," Bortoff says.

Wheels doesn't look so good.

(H-3)

"Nadiyah?" Saraih calls up the stairs.

Ibrahim massages the bridge of his nose, pushing his glasses up over stress-heavy eyelids. "Can you come down here, please?"

"Saraih, can't this wait until the morning?" he asks, fatigue weighing his voice. "After the feast, at least? It's Ramadan; we should be paying homage—"

His wife gives him Her Look. It is just that. Her Look. Neither angry nor sad but void of any sign of emotion. And when she voices what lurks beneath, Ibrahim knows he will regret everything he does from this point on unless he gives in to her. He sighs heavily and waves her forward with a flick of his hand. "Call her again."

"Na-di-yah."

Silence. Now they trade looks. Their daughter may be a strong-willed young woman, but she has never been disrespectful.

"Nadiyah Naji!" Ibrahim yells. *Oh, Nadiyah, please do not do this.* He has never been forced to discipline his daughter. What is the right thing? Ground her? Lock her in her room? Take away her iPhone? Lava boils up from his gut, and he closes his eyes, motioning for Saraih to go up the stairs to fetch their insolent child.

Saraih calls down to him, her voice changing, replacing the burning in his stomach with cold fear. "Ibrahim. We have a problem."

He blinks and runs a hand down his thick mustache.

Saraih pokes her head around the corner of the landing, her eyes conveying a level of scorn he has never seen. It terrifies him. "She's gone." He opens his mouth to speak, but she cuts him off. "Out her bedroom window, Ibrahim. Go after her." He opens his mouth a second time and clamps it shut for good. "Now."

(H-2)

"Who the fuck invited you, again?" Spence ain't feeling it no more. Wheels looks bored. Bortoff is distant. All because this new dickweed kid showed up with his stupid haji-girl. And her, all dressed for emo-sex with her fat ass crammed into her miniskirt and cow-tits spilling out her top. *Bullshit, man!*

"Mike. He goes to my church." Except Dickweed says it with this arrogant pause before "church." Like he's daring Spence to naysay.

"What the hell's that supposed to mean?"

"What?" There again with the gaddamned cocky-ass face.

"Look, junior. You want, we can go outside, but you ain't mouthing off to me in my own crib—"

"Chill." Bortoff grabs Spence's upper arm, firm and

85

comforting. He locks gazes, Spence losing himself in his best friend's eldritch, too-thin blue eyes. Bort cracks a slow-smile, the kind that stretches like a growing fault line and usually leads to a hella fun wild night.

"Thanks, dude." Then turning his attention back to Dickweed, "So who the fuck is Mike? I don't know no Mike."

"Well, he invited us, but we can leave if you don't want party favors." Dickweed thrusts a fist forward and lets gravity unroll a fat quarter-bag. Hydro and so gaddamned green the shit glows with crystals.

"Holy fuck..."

"Wanna re-think the dis—"

The club-darkened room explodes in white. Dickweed yelps and flies into the pressing crowd. Bortoff follows him in, one fist bloodied from Dickweed's flowing nose hole, the other flipping an empty bottle for the kill. "Thunder Troop don't do drugs. Zero tolerance, hooah."

Spence pops his neck and dives in. Wheels gets there first, one of his massive arms wrapping around Bort's waist before he can reach the stupid kid. The haji girl screams and starts to cry.

"Shut up!" Spence yells at her, and then catches something in her face. Familiarity. "No shit," he says, his momentum lost to recognition.

Bortoff hears him and turns his glassy eyes to Spence. "What up?"

"Check her out, dude."

Someone cut the sound system, but *Saving Private Ryan* still fills the overstuffed room with the sounds of war. Spence and Bortoff and everyone else stare at the girl. Her bottom lip quivers, and she rubs her arms.

"What is it already?" Bort asks while Dickweed bleeds from the floor and glares over his pinched nose.

Wheels to the rescue. He maneuvers between Spence and Bort, squaring off with the haji tramp, and then goes all soft.

He puts a hand out. His slur magically vanishes. "Miss, I'm sorry about the... you know. We've just been drinking some, and my friend didn't mean no harm."

She doesn't answer but stops her stupid sniveling. "I'm Jonathan Wheeler. Everyone calls me Wheels. Pretty funny, I guess." He laughs and nods at his chair. Dickweed mean mugs him for hitting on his ugly ass girl. The whole room deflates with Wheels's charm.

Except Spence and Bort. *What the fuck's he doing?* Spence grinds his teeth. "Ma'am, I know how military life can seem kind of harsh and all, but deep down

We're really—"

"I'm a Dependent."

Spence blinks, and the name Mike makes a sizzling, popping synapse connection. Little Memory Game tiles in his drunk head spin a face he recognizes. "Fucking terp," he mutters. Bortoff's smile widens. Something's going down.

Everyone else is immediately thinking the same thing, only on the defensive. Dependent means she is probably some officer's daughter. Insta-shit storm.

"My father is an interpreter."

"He sure is," Bortoff says, advancing on the girl.

Wheels intervenes again, this time taking control the way he used to do when he had legs, guiding the girl and her boyfriend to the front door. Dickweed gives him some shit but agrees to leave, all the way up until they're walking out. He stops and turns to Bortoff, slipping a hand inside his jacket.

"Oh, before I forget," he comes up with a squeeze bottle of amber liquid, like one of those Belly Washer kid's drinks, and squirts it all over Bort.

"FUCK!"

The smell of concentrated ammonia and musk burns everyone's eyes. Urine.

The kid screams, "Infidels!" and runs with his fat ass haji bitch wailing down the hall and out the exit before anyone has time to react.

Wheels rolls eyes over at Bort. And laughs. For some reason, hearing the sound of his voice becomes infectious, and even Bortoff joins in.

Thirty minutes later and Bortoff is wearing one of Spence's clean shirts while his pissy one marinates in the latrine sink. Someone announces they missed last call, and Spence, Bortoff, and Wheels all agree to make a beer run off post since the Class VI can't sell past midnight.

Spence is okay with that, though. The 7-Eleven down from the Fort Lewis Main Gate has a way better selection anyways. Plus, it's a training hot-spot.

(H-1)

"I hate you I hate you I hate you!" Nadiyah screams, flailing her khol-dyed hair through ruined mascara.

"Please, don't say that, baby—"

"I'm not your baby! Dammit, Jeffrey," and she collapses into a puddle on the passenger seat of his Corolla.

Silence stuffs the car thick and palpable. They drive the on-post speed limit of 20mph through the main gate, back to her house.

"I'm sorry," he says. "That was a dick move."

Nadiyah sniffs but keeps her eyes to the reds and greens of traffic lights smearing in the night's drizzle.

"Hey, I'll make it up to you." He leans forward, scratching for her attention.

She rolls her eyes. "What." It's not a question, but much of her fire is already cold embers.

"Buy you a sinfully delicious iced coffee? Your favorite? 7-Eleven's on the way."

She bats thick eyelashes in thought then sniffles again before turning back to her window. "French vanilla. A 32-

oz."

She can practically hear the guilt falling from his shoulders. She closes her eyes and muddles her way through a plan for dealing with her parents. Her iPhone flashes to life with a picture of her father once again, and she swipes her thumb across his neck to silence it.

(H-.5)

Droplets dot the windshield in seven-second blooms before the wipers clear them. Ibrahim listens to his iPhone on speaker. It rings once and cuts short. Again. Voicemail. His daughter's voice sings with the haunting awkwardness of a little girl trying out her first new strides of confident womanhood. Again. Her phone's either out of service in a brick building—like the barracks perhaps?—or she's cut it off.

"Damn it all," he says under his breath, tapping his useless cell against his forehead. The blue display from his car stereo panel reads two minutes to midnight. Nadiyah's been missing over an hour. On a Friday night. Out with an immature boy near—or God help him—*on* an Army base. He sinks and pulls the corner of his phone down to his lip.

Ibrahim eyes the Fort Lewis main gate and creeps through, showing his Government ID to the guard. The streets ahead shimmer from the rain. A siren howls far in the distance. This is a bad night for everyone.

His phone rings through the car system.

"Daddy?" Nadiyah, her voice desperate. "I'm scared—"

Silence.

Ibrahim doesn't think. He fishtails his BMW B7 into the outbound lane toward the siren, a litany of prayers falling from his lips between curses.

(H-hour)

"Pull in here," Bortoff says from the passenger seat. He pops the glove box and takes out Spence's Beretta M-9, 9mm pistol. An exact copy of the Army issue. He drops the magazine, fingers the forward bullet sticking out like a randy dick from the stack, slaps the mag back in place, pulls the slide to the rear and chambers a round. "Thunder Troop Punisher Squad, Green 2: green, Weapons Direct status: red."

"The M9 pistol," Spence recalls from the Thunder Troop Promotions Study Guide, "is a 9mm, semi-automatic, magazine-fed, recoil-operation, double-action weapon chambered for the 9mm cartridge." Spencer keeps his hands at 10 and 2 and caresses the wheel into the turn.

"Keep her straight, driver. Combat park, gear in drive. First BOLO, we snap."

"BOLO," Spence drums his fingers with increasing tempo as his mumbling fact-brain drives his voice louder, "Be On the Look Out. A list of suspect vehicles or personnel often tied to a crime. Adopted from municipal law enforcement and often a combat multiplier in apprehension of insurgent command chains."

"What're we looking for again?" Wheels asks, his voice cracking.

"Beamer. Merc. Toyota with orange panels. You know what those maggots drive," Bortoff says.

Spence eases forward into the empty 7-Eleven lot and slips past the farthest parking space from the door, then pops his black Dodge Magnum power wagon into reverse and backs smoothly into the stall, equidistant from the lines. Like a professional. They've done this too many times to count since getting back. Though this is the first time Bort's opted for "weapons red." They've never pulled his gat before. Spence nods. Tonight's about Wheels. He drops the Magnum into P, engine purring and ready.

"Oh man," Wheels says with a nervous jitter, "What's up with you guys?" He leans forward from the backseat center.

"How about a dry run for some TCP training?" Bortoff turns back to Wheels, and his face melts into a softer smile. "Dude, lighten up. We're just having a little fun. We do this dry-fire shit all the time. Ain't that right, Spence?"

"Hooah."

Wheels falls silent. Distant sirens wail. Bortoff busts out laughing. Spence can't help himself and joins in. Wheels doesn't.

"You guys got issues, man."

Sirens grow louder. Spence squints at Wheels in the rearview, but inside he's calculating flash-to-bang on the sirens.

"Shut up, and take your turn on the gun, Wheels," Bort says. He passes the gat back, and Wheels stammers a bunch of shit but takes it anyway. Like he was bred for it. Spence nods. *Good to have the team back.*

"I'm serious, Spence. I want you to take me back to the B's and my ride. This ain't fun anymore—"

"Sht!" Bortoff leans forward. "First customer," he says in a half whisper.

And damned if it ain't a Toyota with a bad paint job and Dickweed driving. His fat haji girlfriend sits stone cold in the passenger seat, puffy eyes glaring out her water-dotted window.

"Show time."

Before Dickweed can get all parked up right, Spence throws the Magnum in gear and half slides to a reverse blockade behind them, framing them in.

Bortoff and Spence explode from the car and walk up to the Toyota with their hands holding invisible rifles at the low ready, Spence covering Bort from rear guard.

"Get out slow, asshole," Bortoff yells. Spence stands back, aiming his make-believe weapon at the driver while Bortoff closes in for the interrogation.

The kid looks scared. The girl raises her cell, and her face lights from the backglow.

"Shit!" Spence yells.

Two Tacoma PD cruisers screech into an echelon blocking everyone in.

Bortoff hollers, "V-BIED," and raises his hands to aim his not-really-there M-4 Carbine.

The kid in the car cries out something about "Allahu" and "ackbar."

"Bort, get down!" Wheels yells from behind Spence. He fires.

The world erupts in wet confusion, red-white-blue strobes, and gunshot.

Haji girl screams and drops her phone as a bullet flies from behind Spence, striking her in the mouth and pulling her head to her shoulder. The passenger side window explodes out in a shower of safety glass.

Wheels makes a mewling sound overlapped by his vomit splashing against wet pavement.

Four more shots from Tacoma PD spin Bortoff around in a spasmodic marionette's dance. He craters to the ground between the two vehicles.

After an eternal moment filled with the quiet running of engines and rain spatter, one last gunshot, a 9mm, cracks the night, and Spence hears a sound like a wet duffel smacking the pavement behind him. Wheels's chair rolls within his periphery, empty, between their snap TCP and the two police cruisers.

A Beamer slows at the entrance and crawls to a stop, just outside the 100m Escalation of Force mark.

(D+364)

Air heavy with traffic smells of rubber, rust, and wet metal; sea hints stale from old brine and dead mollusks seeping in from the Puget Sound; sugar cookies of sweet, deadly cinnamon. Intoxicating to one man, the aura lingers, trapped beneath the moonlit bowl of Seahawks

Stadium. A lone worker in Seattle Municipal coveralls pulls a pregnant janitorial dumpster to a trashcan.

Abdul Husein Hassan limps on aching limbs. He has aged twenty years in the last one. Something about glycerin exposure. He flexes the three remaining fingers of his left hand, the fingers of his sacred and intact right worrying with nimble precision over wires protruding from beneath a ground level trash can.

"World record for foot racers," he says, his fingers twitching ever so slightly before he regains control, "is held by Patrick Makau at 02:03:38." Hassan applies his disposable cigar lighter's jet to the pre-cut solder chits, fusing wires from a deep recessed package of HME and detcord, to tiny feelers sprouting like roots from the bottom of a GoFone. He applies adhesive and, hunkering down on his knees, fastens the phone to the bottom of the can. He sits back and digs in his pocket, tossing juicy hunks of jerky around the outside. He gives an ejaculating squirt each of mustard and ketchup.

"For the gaddamned dogs." Bomb dogs. Doubtful, but just in case. The sugar and vinegar will mask his work.

He moves to the next point, tugging his overburdened dumpster. Bags of trash ring it like a corndog stick and hot pickle corona. He reaches inside and pulls out another roll of ball bearings, razors, and tiny metal caltrops surrounding an HME core. Modified IED canon. Designed to shotgun out instead of blasting upwards.

"World record for wheelchair races," he recites with rock-steady hands, "is held by Heinz Frei at 01:20:14 in 1999." He looks up from his work and scans the home stretch kill sac. He scoots the roll over another two degrees so the blast will have the largest spread, touching just past the finish line.

"Hey, yo! Spence!"

Hassan jolts and turns to glare over his shoulder at the other stadium janitor. The hyper punk holds out a fist and lets a baggy unfurl. "Let's burn one quick, man. Get one in before the big race tomorrow, huh?"

He squints and a growl starts deep from the back of his throat. As if to emphasize his point, the dope smoker screaming obscenity on the eve of Hassan's ascension hollers from beneath the banner advertising tomorrow's Seattle Marathon. But it's the Special Races he's worried about. Wheelchair division. The race Wheels would never get to win. This brings strength and fire to Hassan. He puffs his chest. He takes a breath and bellows with contempt, "I am Abdul Husein Hassan...Thunder Troop has a Zero-Tolerance Policy, asshole!"

"Your loss, man." The kid disappears out the ground level entrance, leaving Hassan alone to work. He twists the wires to the next GoFone and sets the specific ringtone to his master cell.

He ambles the dumpster up the access ramp to the next tier of trashcans.

Roger Cowin

Units

We live to die,
counting units killed
for Defense Department Spooks
who have never felt a bullet whistle by
two inches from their helmet
or held a friend,
who's cupping his intestines in his hands,
because they were blown out by an IED
they've never looked into
the cold, open bore of an AK-47
nor sighted an enemy down a barrel,
and watched as his head
exploded in a puff of red mist.

After the smoke of battle has cleared,
we count the charred,
bullet ridden corpses of our enemy,
collect their dismembered limbs,
trying not to stare into the faces of the dead,
knowing those same faces
will plague our dreams forever.

We don't do it because we've been forced,
this service is voluntary.
Sign a few papers, pass a physical
and you're trained in the art of death.
We do it because we can, because it's right.
We do it for those who can't,
for those whose lights were extinguished
one sunny, September morning,

whose ghosts still weep for justice.
We do it because we must,
because our business is death
and business is good

Angi Holden

But In This Moment

Later they will wear them threaded through buttonholes,
or at least some semblance of creased petal, leaf and stalk,

a reminder of Flanders fields, the breeze, the Portland stone
engraved with 'Soldier of the Great War' or name and regiment,

faith and service number. But in this moment I only see the fat buds
breaking between the trenches, the rupture of emerald, the burst

of black suns, the tissue folds and I am reminded of you laughing,
leaning back amid the corn rows, your lips as scarlet as poppies.

Jodie English

Viet Nam Draft Lottery,
Cumberland Island, August 5, 1971

Cocooned in our tent
after making love,
a breeze fluttered
the skylight's netting.

We woke to the hooves of wild horses
tearing through sea grass,
the mechanical march
of island armadillo.

As the ocean
drifted towards darkness
we tuned our radio.

Static muddled reception,
wood from our fire
hissed, the sea
kept singing, but then
we heard

the date you were born,
your number,
then silence struck,
the final echo
of a bell long rung.

Sometimes in the well
of morning, I see
your darkness
on the water's skin.

I drink you in.

You're out of range,
deep in that jungle's
great swath of green,
dun flesh
and blank eyes
turning to leaves.

Stuart Keane

Casualty of War

Oh God...what have I done?

Ask any man who his idol is, the one person they look up to the most, and many will respond in the same way. It's almost predictable.

My dad.
My father.
The old man.

A boy's first inspiration is usually his dad. You see it all the time on the playground or the football field. A grown man, pride in his eyes, as he laughs and hollers with a small version of himself while throwing a ball with him or pushing him on a swing. Those moments between a father and son are cherished, sacred.

That first moment of bonding is key; it sets up the relationship going forward. Whether it's a football or playground equipment or even an ice cream cone or hot dog at a baseball game...that moment will always live in your memory.

For me, it was a punch in the face.

That's right, my father showed his love for me with his hands, his alcohol-soaked, wife-beating, adulterous fists. Hands so large that, between gulps of bourbon, they split my lip and my cheek in one swing, spraying blood and enamel across our old refrigerator. Occasionally, they would go lower and knock the wind out of me. I didn't fight back; my physical appearance back then was pathetic, I was weak, I would have been useless in a fight, no match for the behemoth that was my father. I took my beating like a man, always. I never objected or screamed. After all, that's what he wanted, wasn't it? Tough love, I think they call it.

It wasn't just me though.

Sometimes my mother would "fall down the stairs" and interrupt Ed McMahon's nightly diatribe. My father called it falling, but I know he pushed her. It happened about twice a week. Once he broke her arm, and she refused to go to the hospital, not daring to incur more of his wrath. She just huddled on the sofa, blood pissing down her pretty dress, protruding bone glinting in the shine of the low-wattage bulb that passed as lighting in our household—heaven forbid my father should spend money on anything but liquor and smokes.

Later, I found out it was her pride that kept her from going to the hospital. She was a proud woman; she didn't care about strangers thinking ill of her, knowing she was a beaten wife. No, she didn't give a shit about that. She did it to spite him, to show she wasn't weak. It was her way of standing her ground.

I was proud of my mother for that.

It went on seven years, until my father assaulted a police officer. Prison followed. He hung himself in his cell with a blanket. Must have been the loss of his beloved bourbon. We never heard from him, not once. Fucking coward.

After that, my mother and I were alone.

You may find it inappropriate, but I forgive my father for his ways. My mother's abuse was uncalled for; he can rot in Hell for that. You can say he got his comeuppance. No, my father's abuse readied me for my life thereafter. I took care of my mother. I got any job I could find. Paper routes, part-time work at the local store. My mother worked as a waitress to make ends meet. We barely did, our wages paid the bills and left a little for other things. We weren't rich, but we were happy. A family. Nothing would tear us apart again.

Then, one fateful day in 1967, I got my call up.

The Vietnam War came a-beckoning.

Fast forward twenty years, and tears are streaming down my face for the first time in my adult life. I thought I was numb to these feelings; thought I had pushed them to the back of my conscience with the memory of all the horrors I've seen and done.

Looking at the bed beside me, I know I was wrong.

Oh God, what have I done?

Vietnam, and my father, has a lot to answer for.

Now, if I offend anyone by comparing my father's domestic abuse to my participation in the Vietnam War, I apologize. For me, they were very similar. Strategic battlefields, complete opposites in setting, but similar nonetheless. Avoiding my father's beatings or a shot in the head by a fucking Charlie, that was my teenage years.

Like many of my fellow soldiers, I wasn't ready for Vietnam. I doubt anyone was, regardless of distinction. There were the veterans, the people who had experience before their call-up, and the younger soldiers, people with minimal training, those drafted from school, given a crash course, kitted up, an M16 shoved in their hand, propaganda scribed, and ordered to go out and fight. You even had the crazy people who did it for shits and giggles. We were all in the same boat, expected to fight a war we didn't want to fight. Unprepared lambs for the perpetual slaughter.

You don't fight a war that way. Well, you wouldn't think so anyway.

But we did.

I did it. And I survived.

Others weren't so lucky.

As I look in the grimy bathroom mirror now, twenty years later, I still see Rollins over my shoulder, staring back at me. His face is a mess, a hole where his left eye should be, the skull from the eyebrow upwards missing. Blood streams down his face, drenching his uniform and splattering on my bathroom floor. I can barely make out his name on his breast, blood-soaked and muddied. My best friend during the war, we fought together for many a year, slaughtered many a gook that came our way. We saved lives, and we took lives.

I haven't slept properly for seven years. Not a night passes that I don't wake up covered in sweat, screaming at the image of my best friend dying in my arms. I try to shave in the mirror, and although my face is clean and smooth once the razor glides over the coarse bristles, I still feel fragments of his brain sliding down my jaw, a red trail in their wake. The trail breaks at my top lip, slipping down my neck and into my uniform. Blood follows, forced downward by the dousing rain of Vietnam. In the dreams, there's always rain. My bathroom haunts me.

Forced into a waiting helo before the Vietcong could kill me, I couldn't even bring his body with me. As we flew away, firing our last bullets at trees, at hidden snipers and Charlie, I saw Rollins lying there, his blood, face, and brain splattered across the long leaves surrounding him. I saw a fucking gook emerge from the trees, look up at us, hesitate, smile, and then plow another round into my friend's chest for confirmation. Blood sprayed him, and he stole Rollins's boots without another thought. I looked down, vehemence scorching in my veins. My jaw clenched – I thought I would snap some teeth as they pushed against one another – and my skin bristled with absolute fury. I trembled and considered jumping out, landing on the bastard and smashing his face with my rifle butt.

The gunshot is probably the most terrifying thing I ever witnessed in that shithole. Funny, if you consider all I witnessed.

Rollins staring at me is way up there too.

Horrific.

Nightmares. You see things you can't forget.

Like that final gunshot, I'm helpless to do anything.

That gunshot wakes me at night. I call it the 'bourbon blast' because every time it wakes me, I make a futile attempt to drink it away.

Tonight, I wish it would work. Just once.

Operation Firefox was a fuckup from day one.

Rollins and I were a year into our service. Everything up to landing in the jungle is a blur. The first thing I remember is checking out our weapons. I was loading my pistol when Rollins received his M16.

"Hang on a minute. Taylor, this is a second-hand weapon." Scratched into the side was the name JIGSAW. The name didn't ring a bell to me. "How about a new one?"

Taylor, a scrawny bag of bones with bifocals and confidence belying his wiry frame, sneered at Rollins. "It's all we have."

"Really? We're fighting a war, and Uncle Sam can't afford new weapons? What a fucking joke."

"That's the truth. You're lucky you get that one. If you don't like it, write a letter to the president. I'm sure he'll respond in due course," Taylor sneered and looked down at his clipboard.

"So if I take this gun, what's to say it won't get me killed?"

"It's been tested. It's functioning. We had to wash blood and bone fragments out of it, but otherwise, it's fine. Just don't shoot yourself in the face, and you're frosty."

"I don't think Jigsaw said that. What happened to him?"

"I don't fucking know. I'm not your fucking supervisor. Take the gun and fuck off."

Rollins's jaw knotted, but he remained silent. I grabbed his arm and forced him out of the tent. Sand and red flare smoke billowed around us as a helo lifted off. The heat was unbearable as it always was in the early afternoon. Sweat prickled my forehead, the constant itch could drive you to the brink of insanity. From our left, four men ambled over. Our squad. I checked Rollins, who was stripping the M16 apart and checking the innards.

"Sir. Sir." A blond-haired man saluted us individually.

"At ease."

It was Russo. Beside him were Gillicutty, Pearson, and Rogan. Rogan was a teenager, fifteen years old, one of the youngest men I've ever served with. He didn't look a day over it either, his bony frame and blemished skin a dead giveaway. Gillicutty was a stocky fellow with biker tattoos, a bushy beard and a voice deeper than Hades. Pearson was a tall, silent fellow and, as I later found out, a mean shot. The guy had ice running through his veins, a stone cold, calculating killer. He was the most experienced of my new recruits. Uncle Sam would have been proud.

"Can I help you, gentlemen?"

"We're here to join your detail, sir." Rogan's voice had hardly broken, sounding similar to a little girl with a sore throat. I laughed.

"You're joking, right?"

"No joke...sir." Rogan was staring ahead.

"I said at ease, private."

Rogan loosened slightly and looked me in the eye. Abject terror stared back at me. Sure, he did his best to push it down and fit in, but you can't hide fear like that; it's the little voice at the back of your brain. In war, fear is your worst enemy. It can get you killed.

Mind you, I don't blame him. We should all have had that look in our eye. Balls or bravado or utter stupidity, we all thought it would be a piece of cake. We thought we were invincible.

We were wrong.

Operation Firefox was a go.

I look at the bed, not believing my eyes. I fight back tears, turn to the mirror and slide the razor over my face, wiping away a strip of shaving foam. Smooth shaved skin remains. I stare at the mirror and my reflection blurs. For an instant, I see my father, and I wonder why. I haven't remembered his face in years.

I haven't seen him since...since...it eludes me now.

Yet I find myself apologizing.

I'm sorry.

We jumped from the chopper as it landed. Pearson took point, then Gillicutty and Rogan. Russo went last behind Rollins and me. Heat smacked me in the face. Leaves and grass shot up, providing slight cover from any oncoming fire. We didn't receive any on this drop. I once saw a man ripped in half by an RPG blast on a landing. The helo didn't survive. On that occasion, it would be three days before we were rescued, drinking shitty water and nursing a soon-to-be amputee.

He died on the helo on the way out.

That's a story for another day.

The helo lifted away, leaving us on the ground. We merged into the undergrowth and became one with the jungle. Single line formation. Our destination was a small village in the forest west of Da Nang. One of the worst places to be during 'Nam, as it turned out.

The mission should have been simple. The village held a couple hundred people - villagers including kids and women. Innocent people, or so we thought. All we had to do was secure it.

In war, no one is innocent. It's a myth. Innocence is a casualty.

We soon found the village. Drenched in sweat, I swiped my slick forehead on my soggy sleeve. Silence surrounded us, broken occasionally by Rogan sniffing or Gillicutty chewing c-ration Chiclets. We pushed through the trees and staggered into an opening, a lopsided circle of mud dotted along the edge with crooked bamboo huts. A wooden stage sat a few feet off the ground in the center. On it sat food and several tables covered with rice bags and boxes. Two women were tending to the table. A third woman was rocking a baby wrapped in a white sheet. I couldn't hear her, but her lips were moving, cooing to the baby.

The silence was friendly.

I looked around the village and saw mothers bathing children, kids playing with a beaten football. Civilian stuff.

Then there was us, six Americans, armed and dangerous; a certified killer, a biker, a teenager with no pubes, and three soldiers, standing on the edge of their village, encroaching on their territory. When they looked up at us, the glares we got were bona fide evil.

We all smiled, laughed it off, thinking our weapons would buy us some time. Typically we'd walk through the village, do our duty, and leave. No altercation and no aggression. The locals knew the drill. Let the Yanks get on with it. A little give and take allowed everyone to get along.

Sometimes.

A small boy with disheveled black hair and a dirty white t-shirt ran over, yelling something in his native tongue. He headed straight to Russo, who stiffened. He stepped forward and kneeled down. We all started walking around him, heading towards the huts. The kid reached Russo and handed him a card. Russo looked at it, confused. The kid turned and ran back to his mother as she rocked a baby in a makeshift crib. Russo stood up and chuckled. "Jack of Diamonds."

Rogan looked over, lowering his weapon. "Huh?"

"Jack of Diamonds. It's a playing card." He flipped the card between his fingers.

I kept my eyes on the village. "It's a death card. We leave them on the Charlie, so their comrades know who killed them. Bragging rights, if you will."

"Why did the kid give it to me?"

"I don't know, maybe he found it on his gook father and thought it was cool."

Russo laughed. "Creepy shit, if you ask me."

"Happens all the..."

I didn't see the newborn baby flying through the air until it smacked the dirt at Russo's feet. Slow motion took over; the baby's cry distorted in flight, sounding like some deranged battle cry. On instinct, I raised my weapon. The small body rolled over, dead, spraying blood. Russo kicked the body. I heard a metal clunk. "What the..."

The baby exploded.

Russo evaporated in a mist of red and shrapnel, spraying us all with blood and bone. The blast propelled Gillicutty backward, and he crashed into a tree, breaking his back instantly. He slumped in a broken heap in the long grass.

The woman in the center was aiming an AK47 at me.

"Shit," I heard Rogan scream as we all dove for cover. Pearson walked forward, took aim, and blew the bitch's head clean off. Her head was there, and then it wasn't. She dropped onto her table, spilling rice onto the dirt.

Several hut doors opened. Women walked out, armed with rifles. Several children ran out too, armed with knives.

"*Fall back!*"

Gunfire shattered the mundane jungle noises that were so peaceful mere minutes before. Rollins and I retreated to the opening we'd come through and grabbed Gillicutty. We dragged him by his arms as Rogan and Pearson mounted an offense. Gillicutty groaned as we pulled him through the grass, the lush blades whipping him in the face. Female shrieks filled the gaps between the thunders of gunfire. Bullets shredded the trees and leaves around us. Wood and shredded foliage rained down on us. Dirt spat up at our feet, bullets missing us by inches.

If they'd been Vietcong, we'd have all died immediately. With firepower like that, we should've been bullet-ridden corpses. Luckily, these villagers weren't trained in fending for themselves and defending their country from the Yanks they so despised.

You don't get luck like that twice.

We found a felled tree and used it for cover. "Men, mount an offense. Rogan, you and Pearson take left. Rollins, you're with me." I leaned down and slapped Gillicutty. He was alive but severely injured. "Gill, you with me?"

No response. His head was moving, but otherwise he was gone. "Shit."

Bark exploded behind me. I leveled my M16 and took aim. I took out two women and a child who was about to leap at us. His chest exploded in a burst of crimson, and his small frame slapped the tree beside him. The women hurtled to the ground, their guns sprawling beside them. My fellow soldiers were all firing, taking down their attackers.

For a bit, we were winning.

Then Pearson stood up and walked into the open. He took his pistol from his holster and started firing, hitting his target with each shot. Bodies fell one after the other, slapping the blood-soaked mud.

He didn't have enough bullets.

On a reload, a stray Vietcong emerged from the bushes beside us and screamed at him, "*Migook. Migook!*"

In his arm was a long tube attached to a pipe, which spiraled around to a shiny canister on his back.

A flamethrower.

Fire launched into the air with a suppressed roar. To this day, I can feel its heat searing my sweaty brow. Pearson didn't stand a chance. He erupted in a burst of fire and flame. Within seconds, the cloying stench of scorched flesh singed our nostrils and made me gag.

You can train for anything in the forces, but that smell will always get you.

Pearson screamed and flailed, his arms whipping in the air. He ran at the Vietcong and launched himself on his attacker. It took me a second to realize the danger. *"Get down!"*

Pearson smothered his attacker in flame, thus warming the flamer fuel on his back. An explosion tore a hole in the jungle, taking out several maniacal women and children. Bodies erupted and spattered the foliage with blood and bone. A child was whipped into the air, his body snapped across a tree trunk, becoming entangled in the branches. Blood sluiced from his broken body like a demented waterfall. I groaned and stood up, dragging Gillicutty through the opening. Rollins and Rogan followed, the latter was terrified and whimpering.

In the opening, our backs were to the water and mountains. Any imminent threat would come from the war zone we'd escaped. Rollins wound up his radio and called it in. We needed an evacuation chopper.

Distant gunfire told us we weren't out of the woods yet. Literally.

"What do we do?" Rollins was addressing me. He tapped a fresh magazine against his helmet, and then rammed it into the M16. His arms shook.

"We hold off the gooks until the chopper arrives."

"And if we can't?"

"We can."

"But..."

"We can." I looked at Rollins and nodded. Rollins glanced at Rogan, who was on the brink of losing control. He reloaded his gun several times, each time with a full magazine clasped in a trembling fist, and he was chanting incoherent utterings that sounded like a prayer. His flesh was pale except for the odd splash of blood. He stared at the unbridled horror of the Vietnam War. The slaughter and the blood, the death and the chaos. I glanced up at the dead boy in the tree, his neck snapped at an awkward angle. I sighed. Rollins looked at me again and nodded. He understood.

Protect the new guy. His innocence was already dead, though.

"Sir?" Rogan was addressing me now.

"Yes, private?" My eye remained on the tree line, as the gunshots grew ever closer.

"I can't do this."

"You can, private."

"I can't. I can't." Tears streamed down his pockmarked face.

I turned to him and slapped him. "You can, and you will, private. If you don't, a thousand Vietcong are going to burst out of that jungle right there and fucking murder us. They'll shoot us, take out clothes and guns, and probably rape our corpses. They'll kill us all. Our families will never see us again; Rollins here will never fuck his wife again..."

"I don't have a..."

"...and you won't get a chance to see your eighteenth birthday, spend it with your future wife, who is out there. You won't grow up to have a little Rogan of your own, to do your family proud. Are you going to let the VC take that from you? You're not, because we're fucking Americans, okay? We stand and fight until the last. We won't go down at the hand of any fucking gooks."

Rogan nodded. He wiped his face. "Sorry, sir. I won't let it happen..."

An arrow pierced Rogan's face, spearing his eyeball on its tip. Blood sprayed me in the face, and I flinched. Rollins stood up beside me and fired into the jungle. Rogan's teenage body slumped to the ground and rolled down the bank into the river. I looked down at Gillicutty, and he was non-responsive. I kicked his body to make sure.

Nothing.

"Just the two of us, buddy."

But it was the three of us. It was me, Rollins, and the ghost of my father.

The man who'd made it his mission to belittle me, judge me. To stop me from becoming the man I now was. His face was at the corner of my vision, on every enemy.

A distraction, the curse of my family coming back to haunt me at the brink of death.

Then the Vietcong burst through the jungle...

I kneel on the bed, razor in my right hand. I'm shivering, taking in the scene. Slowly, I reach out and take her hand.

I hear my father, in my head. *You did this, boy. Fucking murderer. You're just like me. You love hitting a woman.*

No, I'm nothing like you. I loved her...

Fucking pussy.

My words form as I wipe the tears away. "I'm sorry."

Rollins was killed by Jigsaw's M16. The gun performed what we call 'failure to extract,' which is when the chamber jams on a used shell. This was probably the first thing going through his mind when he signed the gun out. Clean or not, a dead man's rifle is not something you want to inherit. I saw the look on his face as the gun jammed. He looked at me in resignation, knowing he was fucked.

When the left side of his head disappeared in a cloud of blood, seconds later, I went into full-on rage mode. I've rarely felt that way before. My blood boiled, my skin was on fire. I swear my vision turned red, like the fabled saying, but it might have been the blood dripping in my eyes.

I looked at the enemy, staring death in the eyes. The image of my father, his very visage haunting me to this day in every confrontation, miles away from home, in the middle of 'Nam, slowly faded.

He didn't scare me anymore.

I shot a VC as he leapt from the jungle. His head broke open like a melon smashing against a wall.

My father, the distraction, was no more.

I lost control, my entire being – senses, body, motion – went into automatic defense mode. I collected the guns from my fallen comrades and unloaded on that jungle. For a moment, time slowed, bullets were visible in the air. Or at least, it felt that way. Leaves and branches were obliterated. Vietcong, some of them, fell dead in a hail of gunfire. I took four bullets, one to the leg, two in the right arm and one in the left shoulder.

I should have died out there.

I didn't die. My men did.

I led my men to slaughter.

When the chopper collected me, I would have taken their bodies back with me. They had to pry Rollins's mutilated corpse from my arms. I would have died saving the bodies, taken a hundred more bullets. They were honorable men for the brief time I knew them and deserved a proper burial, not to be pilfered and desecrated by the fucking gooks that had taken their lives.

Such was the way in 'Nam.

Rollins stares at me over my left shoulder. His brains slide down my face. It brings back memories of other fights, other battles.

I went back into that jungle a year later.

People say war is hell. What do they know?

Hell is peace compared to war.

Once you've seen a man vanish in a cloud of blood at the hands of a dead newborn child, one who couldn't decide its own fate, mere days into its life, sacrificed at the behest of its mother, nothing is the same.

That's just the beginning.

Torturous images fill my mind. Every day, they chip away at my façade. I'm John Dixon, security guard at the local shopping mall in Denver. I earn enough money to keep my life stable, and there's my inheritance from the war. Payoff money, I call it. It could be hush money for all I care, who'd believe the horrors I've witnessed? Uncle Sam sending me into the backwoods of Vietnam to kill its residents. Yes, I killed them, but who are the real survivors? Me? Rollins's family? Rogan's mother and sister, who were infinitely proud of him for going to war, even though he was shitting his khakis? It's no place for a fucking kid!

In war, there are no survivors. Only victims.

Casualties.

Just like Andrea, my fiancée, who now lies dead in my bed. Strangled because she moved funny in her sleep. The first night she stayed over after our proposal, and I throttled her with my bare hands. Maybe it was a bad dream or something, she was just readjusting in bed and getting comfortable, but my instinct was to throttle her.

She isn't moving...she hasn't for some time.

I don't remember doing it.

I killed the only person who, despite all my flaws loved me for who I am. She didn't give a shit about my past, or how many gooks I shot in the face, or even how many men I led to slaughter. She cared only about me.

Maybe I am like my father after all.

Nothing more than a woman-beating psychopath drunk.

She loved me, enough to marry me. To say yes to my weak, hopeful proposal.

Now she's dead. Sprawled on my bed, naked and cold.

Another casualty of war? Definitely.

I stand here now in the doorway of my bathroom staring at her corpse. She's as beautiful in death as she was in life. I did this. I killed her. I killed an innocent woman because of the images, no, the memories of my time in the war.

Memories I wish I could pull from my brain and flush down the toilet.

I realize my face is half-shaved. The cream still clings to the stubble on the left side of my face. I'm shaving with a corpse on my bed. Habit? Did my brain make me do it to distract me? Do I shave to punish myself for the slaughter of my men, to have Rollins arrive and constantly remind me I got him killed? Rollins nods in the mirror behind me. He's right; I deserve to suffer for eternity. Maybe this is another chapter in that long, slow, tortuous journey to my deathbed, a journey that should have ended in 'Nam, or even at my father's abusive hands, but didn't. Why should I be happy when everyone around me is destroyed by my mere presence?

I toss my razor into the sink with a ceramic clank. I don't even turn around; I toss it over my shoulder as I would a grenade, and it lands perfectly. I move slowly to the bed and sit down, feeling Andrea's leg tap me in the small of my back. I open the drawer in the bedside cabinet and take out my service revolver, placing it on the bed beside me.

I remember holding a young recruit's intestines in with a pot lid. His name I don't recall.

How I smashed a gook's brain in with my rifle and didn't stop until I saw brain ooze from the cracked skull, like some visceral piñata.

The newborn baby flying through the air.

I remember a dream I once had about the baby crawling along the wall, its fragile head twisted around, bloody eyes hanging out on oozing optic nerves, staring at me. I hear blood dripping on the wooden floorboards, tap tapping away, the volume growing. It's screaming for its mother, the woman who so heartlessly tossed it—girl or boy, I don't know—across the jungle to save herself.

This dream is repetitive, routine.

I can't shake it from my *fucking* head.

Once, I was the child, reaching for my father, the man who neglected his family. My eyes torn out, I reached out in vain and my screams went unanswered.

It's one of hundreds in my vivid, traumatized memory banks.

I lift the service revolver off the bed and check the ammo. It's loaded. I glance over my shoulder and look at Andrea. My hand moves to her head and touches her black hair. For the first time since Rollins's death, I'm trembling. I stroke her forehead, noting the coolness, and retract my hand, curling it around the handle of the revolver.

"I'm sorry," I mumble, not able to say or think anything else.

I glance into the bathroom and see Rollins standing there, watching me with his one eye, his arms folded. I see the joker card tattoo on his forearm, the same one I have etched on my skin. I glance down at it, rubbing it with my fingers, and remember the good old days. We were soldiers in arms.

Friends.

I place the barrel tip under my chin. So many people put it in their mouth...that won't work. I want the bullet to go through my brain, not under it.

Once Rollins and I went to a bar after a stressful day. We drank; we ate; we sang badly. Even the women were interested in us, which didn't happen often. I remember asking him what was important in life. He said one sentence that stayed with me the rest of my years.

"Family. You can't sell it, trade it, or lose it. And they always come back."

He was wrong...

I wonder how it would have been with my father, had he bonded with me. Taking his son for his first ball game, his first beer, his first strip club.

I had none of that.

I look up and my father is there, nodding away, smoking a cigar with a cold bottle between two fingers. He rocks back and forth silently, his cold gaze aimed in my direction. He always terrified me.

I haven't seen him since...since...it eludes me now.

No, wait. I remember.

I see his obituary on a crinkled newspaper in my hand. The last time I saw an image of my father. I took it from my mother, who'd been crying over it. I can recall the transparent paper where the tears soaked through. In the corner were two lines of text and a standard photo – no smile – of him, glaring at the camera. He probably wanted to kill the photographer too.

He liked doing that.

He even killed himself.

I look up at his ghost. "I'm not sorry, you got what you deserved."

With that, he vanishes, my demon vanquished.

Family. They don't always come back.

Maybe he could have.

I'll never know.

It wouldn't have changed a thing.

BAM.

"Urgh...where am I...why am I all sticky? What the hell? Is that blood? What was that noise...Oh no, *no, no.* John, *John! What did you do?*"

Neil Davies

The Ten-Year Anniversary

Harry Dixon was a hero. He was a survivor of the British Army's defeat at the hands of Zulu warriors at Isandlwana, feted alongside the heroes of Rorke's Drift as a true British hero of the Zulu War.

And it was a lie.

January 22nd, 1879.

A date that burned fiercely in his memory. Was it really ten years ago? That awful battle? That slaughter?

It did not seem so to Harry. Almost every night he woke in the dark, sweating, crying out in fear as ethereal Zulu warriors attacked him with their *assegais.*

And it did not seem so on the dull, overcast morning of the ten-year anniversary.

An exhausted Harry carefully shaved with cold, soapy water and a near-blunt cutthroat razor. He scraped away the night's stubble and, for a moment, stared at himself in the small shaving mirror. His moustache held flecks of grey, as did his thinning hair. His face was creased, his forehead heavy with frown lines. His eyes were dull.

He could not remember the details of *that* day; only a blurred memory of the terrifying attack by the Zulus, and then his stumbling into Rorke's Drift, later that same day. What happened during the battle, how he had managed to fight off the Zulu and escape the slaughter of his fellow soldiers, he could not remember.

They called him a hero, because he survived. A nagging guilt at the back of his mind told him there was nothing heroic about *how* he survived. He wished he could remember, even though he feared what had remained hidden for a decade.

On leaving his lodgings, and with the London stone beneath his feet forming a solid and, more importantly, safe foundation, he grew more sure of himself. The background noise of the city, horses' hooves on cobblestones, street vendors' cries, all helped to drown out the doubt and guilt in his mind. Someone would know the truth. Or perhaps *he* would finally remember. If he did, would he reveal his own guilt to the assembly of *true* heroes? Or would he continue to hide, to play the part the newspapers had thrust on him even before his return to England?

Up ahead, a typical London fog drifted into the streets, dropping a grey shroud over the people and the buildings.

What's that?

The background noise had taken on the rhythmic pulse of a Zulu chant. Voices rose. Assegais slammed shields of animal hide in perfect synchronization, each beat driving into his heart, his belly. He could almost see them, running over the hills, a black wave of power and death.

Fear squeezed his chest. Sweat blossomed on his face. How could he escape? Where could he hide? Where could he run?

This time.

The thought brought reality sweeping back. He was in the city once more, with city sounds and city sights. No Zulu chants. No attacking army of warriors.

I ran while my fellow soldiers fought and died.

He was certain of it, the guilt heavy in his stomach. How could he go through with this reunion when, other than *being* at Isandlwana, his story was a lie?

The same sounds of the city he had found so reassuring now seemed to crowd in on him, rising in volume, making other thoughts almost impossible. Streets that had seemed almost empty now buzzed with people, talking, shouting, pushing.

He needed to get away, to escape. A place to be on his own. To think.

Trying to return to his lodgings, he found the way blocked by phantom shapes that swirled and darted in the growing fog. They may have been people. They may have been ghosts. He could not tell.

An alley lay opposite. He ducked inside and sat in its deep shadow, his breath blowing heavy, his nerves straining, ready to snap.

Why don't they all go away? What do they want of me?

He could never understand why they had not formed a *laager* when they camped in the shadow of the sphinx-like hill, Isandlwana. The circling of wagons had been standard procedure on similar expeditions in the past, but apparently, the order had come from Lord Chelmsford himself. There was no arguing with that. Chelmsford knew what he was doing. He presumably had his reasons. But it was an oversight that worried Harry and some of the other soldiers.

Chelmsford surprised them again when he rode out of the camp with, it seemed, a good half of the men. He left behind soldiers of the 1st Battalion, including Harry himself, and some of the 2nd. There were others too, mostly a native contingent. The talk was that Chelmsford was off to crush the Zulus, and that was fine by Harry. He had no particular wish to face the enemy. Not that he doubted the superiority of the British soldier, with his Martini-Henry rifle and his training. But the natives frightened him. The Zulus were rumored to be fierce fighters.

He wished Chelmsford every success. He wanted to go home in one piece.

"You think his Lordship is doing the right thing?" said Sid Morehouse, a friend from the parade ground back home.

"I *hope* His Lordship is doing the right thing," said Harry. "Otherwise we're all in trouble."

Sid nodded and wiped sweat from his forehead.

"I can understand why the natives go about with next to no clothes on most of the time," he said. "Far too bloomin' hot in this country."

"Makes you nostalgic for a bit of London fog or good old English rain," said Harry.

"Pulleine's been left in charge," said Sid, lowering his voice to a whisper. "Does that make sense to you?"

"He's a Lieutenant Colonel," said Harry. "Don't suppose Chelmsford could ignore him in the chain of command."

"But Pulleine! He's a pen pusher. He doesn't know how to command troops in the field."

"He won't need to will he?" said Harry. "Chelmsford will break the Zulus and we won't have to do anything."

"Do you really believe that?"

Harry looked across the bustling camp, British and native soldiers, some civilians tagging along, wagons haphazardly strewn about. He *had* to believe they would not be attacked. He was scared just being in Zululand. Anything more was too terrifying to contemplate.

"Harry? Are you okay?"

Harry, still crouched in the shadows of the alley, looked up and, for a moment, failed to recognize the speaker who stood nearby. He looked closer.

"Sid? Sid Morehouse?"

"Yes Harry, its Sid," said the figure, moving closer. "I saw you duck into the alley here, but I wasn't sure it was you at first. Why are you hiding?"

"I get a bit jumpy," said Harry, grateful to talk to someone who could understand. "Don't go out much these days."

"Do you still have nightmares?"

"Yes, almost every night."

"Me too," said Sid. "Sometimes it seems like my whole life is a dream, a nightmare."

"It doesn't go away," said Harry. "I don't remember that much, but the images...the Zulus attacking...men dying..."

"It's okay," said Sid. "I understand Harry. I'm the same myself. It never goes away."

The two old comrades fell silent. Sid slid to the alley floor alongside Harry.

"You going to the reunion?" said Harry after some time.

"I don't think so," said Sid. "It's mostly the lads from Rorke's Drift. You were there though. You going?"

"Probably," said Harry, growing thoughtful. "Now that you mention it, I don't remember seeing you at Rorke's Drift, Sid. Where did you go after you escaped Isandlwana?"

"Harry," said Sid, as a sudden gust of wind swirled dust into the air of the alley, into Harry eyes, forcing him to close them for a moment. "Who ever said I escaped?"

Harry opened his eyes, rubbing the grit from them, and turned to ask Sid what he meant. But Sid was no longer there. Harry was, once again, alone in the alley.

He shivered, knowing Sid could not have left without him knowing, without him hearing something. A cold finger of fear ran the length of his spine and tickled the base of his neck. He thought he heard a distant sound of Zulu drumming.

Harry, as much as he shunned the companionship of his fellow man, felt a sudden urge to be among them once again. He did not want to be alone in a dark alley. He pushed to his feet and almost ran into the street. It was not busy, but there were some people about, enough to help him regain a semblance of control.

Sid Morehouse was nowhere to be seen. Harry was not surprised.

When the attack came, Harry and Sid fought alongside

each other.

Lieutenant Colonel Pulleine organized his defense as best he could, faced with the unexpected full force of the Zulu army of over twenty thousand well-organized warriors. Slowly the British line was forced back, closer to the camp. The Zulu attack formation, the traditional horns and chest of the buffalo, stretched the British defence, with the right-hand side finally giving way. Zulu warriors swarmed into the camp and the hand-to-hand battle was joined.

Chants and calls of the attacking warriors mingled with screams of the dying and the clatter of gunfire. Gun smoke from the Martini-Henry rifles drifted across the battlefield, clouds of desperation and despair. Swords clashed with assegais. Hands grappled hands. Men died on both sides, but as the battle progressed, more and more red-uniformed bodies littered the ground.

Harry and Sid had been forced back, towards the rear of the camp. They stood back to back, surrounded. With no ammunition left, they used their rifles as clubs, beating back Zulu warriors with desperate swings. *Assegais* stabbed towards them, never quite reaching the two bloodied, sweat and grime covered British soldiers. The rifles grew heavier with each swing, the heat even more overpowering. Harry felt dizzy, disoriented. He dropped his rifle.

An assegai found his side, ground into it. Through the white-hot pain, he felt it inch farther in, then suddenly pull back. The pain burst in sharp, jagged lines from the wound, spreading throughout his body. A terrible weakness accompanied it, making his hands shake and his legs tremble.

He saw, through bleary eyes, a Zulu warrior lunging towards him. By instinct, he grabbed at a surprised Sid and pulled him across. The *assegai* plunged deep into Sid's stomach.

As he fell, Sid looked up at Harry. He could not speak

through the blood already bubbling from his lips, but the eyes were full of shock, of questions.

Harry could only stare in silence. He had no answers, no excuse other than fear and cowardice. As Sid's body twitched, already more dead than alive, despair and disgust battled with a tenuous sanity in Harry's mind. Had he sunk so low that he would betray a friend? *Murder* a friend?

He continued to stare as Sid's eyes glazed over, the last threads of life drifting away. In a moment of brutal clarity, Harry knew the betrayal had been ultimately worthless. What had he gained by avoiding one assegai when so many more waited to kill him? His soul was surely damned to an eternity in Hell. There seemed no point in delaying its journey. He gathered what little courage he had left.

"Come on then!" he screamed, closing his eyes, waiting. "Just do it. Get it over with."

But no thrust came. No killing blows.

Cautiously, he opened his eyes.

The sky had darkened, a shadow falling across the battlefield. A solar eclipse had brought premature night to the bloody camp.

For one moment, Harry hoped the Zulu warriors would be frightened by the sudden darkness, perhaps even run away. But they did no more than the remaining British soldiers. They looked at the sky. They continued to fight.

Perhaps that small delay was all Harry needed.

He was about to run when a Zulu stepped in front of him. But this was no warrior.

A Sangoma stood before him, goat bladder tied at the back of the hair, a belt of snakeskin around his waist. He flicked a cow-tail whisk and pointed at Harry.

Witch doctor, thought Harry. *Why don't they just kill me?*

The Sangoma spat words at him in Zulu, chanted and danced around him while the warriors stood and watched. He thought he saw pity in some of their stares.

He made a break for it. *Assegais* were raised, but a shout from the Sangoma froze them in place. Harry was not stopped as he ran from the battlefield, chased by the darkness as the sun reappeared in the sky.

"You really believe a Zulu witch doctor put a curse on you?" said Sid, as Harry finally stumbled his way back into his lodgings.

Harry stopped, dropping his keys onto the threadbare carpet. His army colleague stood by the small window, the light seeming to almost pass through him, illuminating him from within.

"You're dead," said Harry, his voice breaking. "I saw you die at Isandlwana."

"I may be dead," said Sid. "But you're the one who thinks he's cursed."

"I can't be talking to you," said Harry as he sat in a chair and covered his face with his hands. "It's not real. I'm going mad."

"Speaking of *mad*," said Sid. "I wasn't exactly pleased when you killed me!"

The shock of the accusation stung Harry into pulling his hands from his face.

"The Zulus killed you."

"You used me as a shield so they killed me instead of you."

The truth weighed heavy, and Harry hung his head in shame.

"I was scared. I didn't think."

"I'm not here for an apology," said Sid, still standing at the window, never moving. "Nor am I here for revenge. It's been ten years, Harry. The Zulu Nation is gone, its people scattered. You weren't cursed by the witch doctor. You were cursed by your own guilt."

"The nightmares," said Harry, groaning. "Every night, the nightmares."

"You were meant to die that day, just as I did. But the witch doctor interfered after I was killed and decided it would be more cruel to let you live with your memories, rather than simply die at the point of a spear."

"Ten years," said Harry. "Ten years of being frightened to go to sleep."

"You're so tired you're seeing things, hearing things."

"Like the drums, the warriors. And you!"

Harry, still staring at the carpet, waited for a response. Silence. Slowly he looked up, towards the window. For a moment he thought he saw a figure standing there, but it was just the sunlight, the curtains and shadows. He was alone.

He hung his head back down and cried.

"Surely ten years is enough suffering for one man," he said through his sobs.

In the distance he heard drums, chanting, the banging of assegais on shields.

He stood and turned.

Where there should have been a wall, there now stretched the open plains of Zululand. Some distance behind him rose Isandlwana, where the bodies of his fellow soldiers lay, cut open by the Zulu warriors so their spirits might be free. Against the bright sky, the hill gave no clue as to the bloody battle that had been fought there, the battle Harry had run from.

He turned again as the rhythmic banging and chanting rose in volume, becoming almost deafening.

A dust cloud on the horizon hardened into thousands of Zulu warriors, charging towards him. Already the flanks were moving out into the classic pincer formation. If he did not move quickly, the horns of the Buffalo would close around him and he would be trapped.

Chelmsford was a fool to underestimate the Zulus.

Harry knew that now, ten years on.

He ran, away from Isandlwana and towards Rorke's

Drift, where he might be safe, because the battle at Rorke's Drift was a victory for the British. The soldiers stationed at Rorke's Drift were heroes. He was a hero too, because he threw his friend on a spear to save himself and then ran away. As he ran now.

The warriors were closing. Soon they would be within throwing distance and Harry tensed himself, ready for an assegai to hit him in the back. It never came, but the battle cries of the warriors did. Loud. Deafening.

Other sounds intruded. Puzzling, out of place sounds. Running footsteps on wood. People talking as though nothing was happening, as though it was just another day.

He risked a glance back. The warriors were closer again. He saw their enraged faces, the assegais raised, ready to strike. They were angry he had evaded them for ten years. But now they could finally kill him.

He ran. He heard a horse, a shout, but could only see the African plains and the onrushing Zulus.

"He ran right out into the road, he did," said the cab driver, red faced, flustered.

The Police Constable nodded and wrote everything down in his notebook.

"And I suppose you would have had no chance of stopping," said the Constable, without looking up from his notes.

"The horse was on him before I realized it," said the cab driver. "The beast panicked, pulled the cab on. I felt the wheels bump over him, I did." He shuddered at the memory.

The Constable looked at the twisted, bloodied body of Harry and saw wheel marks across his broken head, running down his body. Somehow, the wheel had sliced him open. His guts leaked from the wound.

"Poor man just wasn't looking," he said. "I don't think there's any doubt this was a tragic accident."

"I wonder who he was," said the cab driver.

The Constable shrugged. It did not seem to matter.

And if anyone heard the faint sound of drums, of chanting, of *assegais* clattering against shields in the distance, they did not say anything. Nor did they speak if they heard a distant cry for help, as though from a disembodied spirit, carried away by those who had liberated it.

Ten years of nightmares were over. An eternity lay ahead.

D. Thomas Minton

Portraits from the Shadow

When Trung disembarked at LAX, the dead began whispering to him. In the underground tunnel connecting the international terminal to the domestic one, the spirit of a young woman whimpered from the murky shadows. He tried to console her, but managed only to attract the attention of a uniformed man who told him to move along. In Denver, the ghost of an angry teen hissed at him as he stepped off the rental car shuttle. All along the lonely road twisting up through the forest of snow-capped pines, lost spirits glared at him from the edge of the blacktop. America, like Vietnam, had a problem with ghosts.

Trung was thankful when he arrived at Hampton McElvy's cabin and found no spirits haunting it. His fingers ached as he released the steering wheel and sat quietly, trying to collect himself. He had traveled halfway around the world to speak with McElvy. What if the man couldn't help him? Trung wasn't sure he could handle another disappointment.

He touched the pocket of his jacket. The crinkle of the paper within reassured him and he dismissed thoughts of failure.

After several deep breaths, he climbed onto the porch and rapped quietly on the plank door. The hinges creaked; an eye squinted out through the narrow crack.

"I don't give interviews anymore," McElvy said, his drawl like John Wayne. To Trung, every American sounded like John Wayne.

The door started to close.

"No interview," Trung said, putting his hand against the wood. He removed the yellowed rectangle of newsprint from his pocket and held it up for McElvy to see.

"I don't talk about that anymore," McElvy said.

"Please, I came from Vietnam to speak to you."

The eye blinked at him.

"I am hopeful you can tell me about this man," Trung said. "He is my father."

Trung set the clipping on the table between them. Three weeks ago, he had found it among his mother's things after her funeral. He had never seen a picture of his father before, but his uncle had confirmed the identity of the man in the newspaper photo.

McElvy studied his knuckles as his knobby fingers worked them over. Life had taken a knife to his face and carved fissures around his eyes and across his forehead. "Ask what you need to ask," he said.

Even with the wood fire in the stove, a chill clung to the room.

"My name is Nguyễn Hiếu Trung. I am from Vietnam. For twenty years I have searched for my father's spirit so I can bring it home, but I cannot find him. Do you remember this man?"

McElvy's mouth twitched. It looked to Trung like he was having a conversation with himself.

Trung shifted in the wooden chair. He thought about the money he had spent to get there and was starting to regret his decision. Impulsive and wasteful, he chided himself. Maybe his uncle had been right after all. Why would an American remember a single North Vietnamese soldier he had photographed over forty years ago?

"I remember 'em all," McElvy said, his voice barely audible. "They don't let me forget..."

"In January of '68, I volunteered to go to Vietnam as a stringer for the Associated Press. If you wanted to make a name for yourself, that's what you did. I was fresh off the tarmac when the North launched the Tet Offensive. They took the ancient city of Hué, about fifteen miles north of where I was housed with the 5th Marines.

"Hué was crawling with NVA. Bullets and bombs. Booby traps everywhere, and not the kind that killed you fast, but the kind that took off a foot or a hand or cut you deep enough you'd bleed to death 'cause they couldn't get choppers in with all the heat.

"I spent two weeks thinking I wouldn't see another day. I slept next to bodies, with their stink for a blanket. When I ate my rations, I ate death. At night, we'd hole-up in some dark building, and we'd hear screaming and groaning outside. Sometimes in English, sometimes not. Nothing we could do. We learned that lesson quick, when a marine tried to help a little boy burned by napalm. He took a bullet in the neck and screamed until he finally died. Seemed like it took an hour, but couldn't have been more than a minute. We couldn't get to him; all we could do was watch and listen, listen to him gurgling and weeping, as he bled into his lungs.

"Lance Corporal Stillman. Nineteen. He had a girl back in Omaha and a baby on the way who would never see his daddy."

McElvy's Adam's apple slid up and down his long throat like a yo-yo on a string. "You can't learn to survive something like Hué," he said. "It was sheer dumb-ass luck who came home and who didn't."

Outside, the day darkened as snow began to fall. The yellow light from the overhead bulb huddled around the two men, as if it was afraid to venture into the room's darkening corners.

"We lost a lot of good people over there, but then, so did you."

Every person Trung knew had lost family members in the war: fathers, mothers, brothers, sisters, millions of

Vietnamese people. Many of them had never been found or properly buried, leaving their ghosts trapped in the shadow between the pain of the living and the peace of the afterlife. As long as their loved ones were lost, the living had failed their ancestors and would not prosper.

Trung had devoted his life to using his gift to reunite families with their lost dead, or just as often, the dead with their lost families. After years of searching, he had never been able to find the one ghost he truly needed to find.

McElvy's bloodless-white knuckles gripped the edge of the table. "In Huế, I was sure death was looking for me," he said. "I couldn't have been more right and more wrong."

"The day after Stillman died, we got lit up by the NVA. In that craziness, I became separated, which is not a good place to be with nothing but a Nikon F. Not knowing what else to do, I ran. No care for where.

"I ran until I got my wits back enough to realize running like that would do nothing but get me killed. I ducked into a building that at least had walls and a roof. I found a dark corner and sat there and shook and shook. Couldn't stop myself.

"About that time I saw him. He came through the doorway. A marine, young, face smeared with dirt and paint, all quiet like. He squatted next to me and leaned on his rifle like it was a walking stick. That's when I recognized him.

"I thought I was hallucinating or maybe it was his brother. I didn't know. I said, 'Is that you Stillman? You okay?'

"He had this look on his face, serene, like the world no longer mattered, like he was beyond it all, aloof. Yet I could see a sadness in the tilt of his eyes and the way he looked past me, like watching something far away, something wonderful he could never reach.

"I touched his arm to get his attention. It was cold,

unnaturally cold, and my stomach dropped out of me like I fell out of an airplane.

"I did then what I was trained to do. I took his picture. I shot his face wide open at a thousandth, because of the light. Soft on the edges, but the eyes were sharp enough to see right into his soul. Right in, like lookin' down a well. Then he stood up.

"I hissed at him to stay down or Charlie might see him, but he didn't need to worry about that anymore. He paused in the doorway he'd come through and motioned for me to come with him. Then he was gone."

McElvy's mouth worked like he was chewing a piece of gristle. "I saw Stillman die, but there he was."

Realizing he hadn't been breathing, Trung drew a sharp breath. He couldn't decide if McElvy was telling the truth or if the stress of combat had caused him to see things. Vietnam was full of spirit mediums who claimed to have the gift to commune with the dead, but in Trung's experience, few people really had the gift for it. Most were charlatans taking advantage of people's need for closure. "In Vietnam, we believe the dead can haunt the living. They can be helpful or they can hurt you. Vietnam is a land of ghosts, many from the war with America, and we cannot forget the lost ones. To do so dishonors them and dishonors us."

McElvy looked up from his hands with weary eyes.

The room seemed cold enough to crystallize the old man's breath, but only words came out of his mouth.

After Stillman went through that door, I sat there for a long time trying to figure out if I was hallucinating. It crossed my mind that maybe I was already dead, and to be honest, to this day I don't know if I am or not.

But I was a photographer, a journalist, and my curiosity wouldn't let me be.

As I neared the doorway, I heard a droning sound. Some light came in through a hole on that side of the building, so I could see into the other room. It was filled with flies, everywhere, like a cloud of black pebbles. The biggest flies I've ever seen, but then, with all them bodies, what did I expect?

Must have been two, three hundred of 'em, laying on the ground like knocked over bowling pins. Women still clutching little kids, old men with their hands tied behind their backs. Many of them gaped up at me appalled, like I'd crashed some private party. They was all shot in the back of the head, execution style.

I just stood there, looking, 'cause I didn't know what else to do, and that's when I saw her. A young woman, movie-star beautiful. Sitting there with no expression I could read on her face, sort of like she had no opinion one way or the other about what had happened. She looked through me, with eyes like Stillman's—far away. The pupils big, so I could see right into them. I could see flashes of who she was, her life, like little vignettes played out with shadow puppets.

My hands were shaking so much, I could barely lift my camera, but when I got it up to my eye, everything just changed. My hands went rock-steady. Without thought, they worked my Nikon's settings; f/16 at a thirtieth, because I wanted to see every strand of dark hair framing her face. I shot only one picture; then she got up and left. As she did, an old man sat down in her place. I shot him from slightly above, f/4 at one-five hundredth, so his face would rise from the bodies beneath him.

More came. Kids with their mothers, men not fit to fight, more women, some beautiful, some not. I never changed film; it never occurred to me. I just kept shooting and shooting and shooting, picture after picture, and then they'd get up and leave and go someplace, I don't know where because someone else always sat down. I took pictures until it got too dark.

Then everything got quiet. No flies, no explosions, no screams. Just quiet.

For the first time since entering Hué, I felt at peace.

I sat in that room all night, so dark I could see nothing. The stink must have been incredible, but the whole damn city stank, so I didn't notice.

I saw him with the first light. Where he came from, I don't know. He sat among the bodies, like a heron in a rice paddy. Sat there, perfectly still. He wore a NVA uniform, and scared me so much I nearly pissed myself. But then I saw his face, and I knew I had nothing to fear. I saw what looked like regret, maybe for things done, or maybe not done.

We sat like that until the dawn moved across the floor and put light on him. Then I took his picture. It was the last one I remember taking.

McElvy held the yellowed newsprint in his trembling hands. "I photographed your daddy wide open at a thirtieth. It never should have come out," he said, "but he wouldn't be denied."

Trung's body thrummed. If he could find the building, maybe he could find his father's spirit, not to mention the hundreds of others that likely still haunted that killing ground. "Where was this place?"

McElvy shrugged.

Trung's face flushed hot. How could McElvy dismiss his question? Trung restrained himself from raising his voice. He was in McElvy's home, and as an American, McElvy could not understand the importance of bringing lost spirits home. Trung lowered his eyes as he tried to balance his challenge with a show of respect. "You must help me find that building."

"It wasn't far from the place they call the Citadel, but I can't say more. Getting there was crazy. Getting out, I was crazy. A group from the 5th Marines found me seven days later, still sittin' there. They heard my camera clicking, and pried it out of my hands, so I was told some days later. I don't remember any of it after that first night. Finding that building doesn't matter, though, because he ain't there. None of them are there anymore."

Trung exhaled a sharp breath. He closed his eyes and concentrated on slowing his pulse. What did this American know? It didn't matter that the bodies were no longer there; the bodies were not important.

McElvy grabbed Trung's wrist; his cold fingers sucked away any warmth remaining in Trung's arm. "He ain't there." McElvy's eyes had a wild gleam.

Trung pulled his arm away. His chair scraped back several inches with the sudden motion. He had seen that same glint in the eyes of some of the Vietnamese veterans, the ones who hadn't been able to leave the war behind.

"There ain't no rhyme or reason," McElvy said. "Why does one man die when his buddy next him lives? What makes good men do bad things?" McElvy rose. In the sepia halo of light, he seemed much taller than Trung remembered. "You came all this way to find your daddy, didn't you?" He retreated into the shadows lingering at the room's perimeter. He stopped at a door Trung had not noticed before.

McElvy tugged at the bolt with his knobby fingers until it gave.

Trung rose and backed away. "What's in there?"

McElvy pulled the door aside. The opening was a black rectangle etched on the darkness. Without answering, McElvy stepped through the doorway and was gone.

Silence settled on the room like a snowfall. Trung hugged his arms and shivered. Out the window, snow collected on the windshield of his rental car. At the rate it was sticking, the road would soon be impassable, and he would be trapped here. Trung became uncomfortably aware of how little he knew about McElvy or his prejudices.

Trung picked up the newspaper clipping and stuffed it into his pocket. McElvy had admitted he had nothing else he could tell him about the whereabouts of his father. If he left now, he could at least get back to a road that might still be clear of snow. But Trung had crossed the world to learn everything he could about his father. Was there anything else McElvy could tell him? If there were anything more, no matter how small, he could not leave.

Trung stopped at the doorway through which McElvy had disappeared. Cold air, like that from a meat locker, blew through the opening and sent a violent shiver through his entire body. After several long seconds, his eyes adjusted to the dimness of the narrow room, its windows covered with thick oil cloths to block out the light.

McElvy stood before a bank of file cabinets. The mist from his breath swirled around his head as he spoke.

I spent a month in a hospital in Saigon; then I left Vietnam. I gave my film to the AP, and told them I was done. When I got home, I put my camera in a box and tried to go about my life, but you don't just go back to life after that. You don't just shower away that kind of filth.

I started hearing voices, soldiers, woman, crying babies, English and Vietnamese and God knows what else. I thought I was going crazy. They came from my closet. When I opened the door, I would hear them like they were hiding in the pockets of my shirts. I pulled my closet apart, looking everywhere for them. My shoes. The pockets of my pants. The boxes of junk. Then I found my Nikon. The voices were coming out of it. I opened the back and inside was a roll of film.

I'm sure I gave the AP all my film, every last bloody roll of it. Yet there it was, and as I held it in my hands, I heard the voices so loud in my head, all talking at me so I couldn't separate any single one, like I was in a huge crowd, and all of them were clamoring for my attention.

I cleared out my dark room and developed the roll, but the film was blank, until I made the prints. Then I saw the faces. The first one was Lance Corporal Stillman. When I touched his print, I heard his voice in my head, clear as if he were standing next me and speaking into my ear. He told me about how much he missed his wife, and how sorry he was he would never see his baby grow up. He begged me to find them and tell them he loved them. He begged me to take him home.

I promised him I would.

I printed photo after photo, hundreds of 'em, all from that blank roll of film. Each portrait spoke to me as I printed it and hung it to dry. There were more faces than I remembered from that room. There were soldiers, both American and Vietnamese, more civilians, more children, more women and men. Hundreds upon hundreds like everyone who died at Huế had lined up for their portrait.

Sometimes they asked me to find their parents or husbands or wives. Sometimes they begged me to tell their story. Sometimes they just cried, and I couldn't understand what they wanted. Most I couldn't understand, 'cause I don't speak Vietnamese.

I kept my promise to Stillman. It took me months to find his widow. When I told her why I was there, she slapped me across the face and slammed the door on me. I slipped the portrait underneath. As I let it go, I felt Stillman's presence leave in peace. He was home, and he seemed to know it.

As I walked away, the door opened, and she stood there, tears on her face, holding my picture in one hand, Stillman's baby in the other. She didn't say anything to me, but I could see everything I needed to see in her eyes.

McElvy pulled open a drawer of the file cabinet. Stuffed inside were old manila envelopes.

Trung came forward, as if reeled into the dark room by a string. He felt an energy emanating from the drawer. At first it rose from the tattered envelopes like a murmur, but as he drew nearer, it grew louder, like a crowd awakening from a long sleep. In the noise, Trung heard voices, jumbled together like noodles.

"I tried to find them all," McElvy said, "but I didn't even know where to start. In '76, I went back to Saigon--Hồ Chí Mihn City--not an easy thing to do at that time. With the help of a Vietnamese art dealer, I hung pictures in some galleries, hoping someone would recognize them, hoping someone would hear something and believe me. Your daddy's picture was one of them. But I got nothing."

Trung's hand hovered over the envelopes. Goosebumps rose on the back. Without thought, he reached into the drawer and pulled out an envelope. It took both hands to work it free.

"I took good care of them," McElvy said, "as well as I could, but they want to go home. They need to go home."

Trung's fingers shook so much he had difficulty unwinding the thread holding the flap closed. He slid a glossy print halfway out. His father's eyes, stared at him. He looked younger than he had ever imagined.

"I--" Trung's voice cracked in his throat. He pressed the photograph against his cheek, unable to speak. The picture smelled of mildew and age, but it was warm against his skin, like a parent's comforting hand. Trung closed his eyes and imagined what his life would have been like with his father. His uncle had done as well as he could, but sometimes a boy simply needed his father.

"It's me; it's Trung," he whispered in Vietnamese.

"I'm sorry," his father said gently into his ear.

Trung held the picture out and looked again into the eyes. They were crisp and clear, the edges pulled with sadness.

"If only I had obeyed, I would have been there for you,"

his father said.

In his father's eyes, Trung saw the room in Huế, the hundreds of unarmed people kneeling with their backs to a line of Vietnamese soldiers. Over the crying children and women, a Vietnamese officer screamed at the soldiers to rid Vietnam of the imperialist sympathizers. When the soldiers hesitated, the officer drew his pistol and shot the soldier nearest him who had lowered his rifle. As he bullet ripped through his father's head, the line of rifles popped and rattled.

Trung screamed out, the picture crumpling in his hand. He pressed it to his forehead and wept.

The photo in Trung's shirt pocket warmed his chest as he loaded the last of the sealed boxes into the back of the rental car. As he let go of the door, the voices faded but did not go away.

Trung turned to McElvy standing in the snow to the side. He bowed to the old man. "I owe you--"

McElvy took his hand. "No," he said, and pressed a wad of green bills into Trung's palm. "To help."

Trung looked at the money. He had done nothing to deserve it, but to give it back would be an insult. He would earn the money he decided. "I will find their families," Trung said, knowing it was what McElvy needed to hear.

The lines around the old man's eyes softened.

As Trung pulled out onto the snowy road, the murmuring in the back of the car grew animated. The dead knew their journey home had finally begun.

G.L. Helm

Lucifer on Air Strikes

The jets! How beautiful they are!
Like arrows thirsty for hearts blood.
Birds so smooth in flashing speed
That flesh and feathered beasts
Which fly by hearts labor are nothing!
These other birds, these jets --
They fly by fire!
They consume in rav'ning gulps so swiftly taken
They are passed before they can be seen.
Those other birds just live --
Sowing seed of grass and flower
Which grow and bend beneath the driving wind.
And they continue!
They renew themselves and all the filthy grass
Which greens the earth --
But the other birds -- the jets --
The flowers that they sow do not renew.
They burst and roar and spread on gusts of wind
which they create
When Napalm blooms upon the waving grass.
A wind which bends all things before it,
And carries a perfume so sweet it cannot be forgot
Through all eternity.
Ushered in with orange and crimson petals
They bring eternity, the jet sown flowers,
Of delicate devouring flame as ravenous for earth
As streaking jets are hungry for the sky.
Wondrous birds! Delicious blossoms!
Reeking buds in damnation's door yard
Carried to the earth on back swept wing

With blazing hearts and empty souls.
And when the fires bloom I smile
Remembering that when living creatures burn
I am near O men--
I am marvelous near.

David S. Pointer

Stratocruising the Turbocompound

Christmas creep, oozed-in, like
a double needle nightmare
all inner glow, elsewhere,
an underfunded-heroine-type
experienced cabin pressure,
sortie-consciousness, as tank
barrels drooped down far as
elephant trunks, thirstily
from the electromagnetic pulse
the aerodynamic drag inside
ever expanding, war coin purse
cauterizing
guzzling
Archimedes
ever expanding, war coin purse

Strider Marcus Jones

Nuclear Toys for Nuclear Boys

Nuclear toys for nuclear boys
In khaki, blue, green and grey;
Action men with meccano kits
Remorseless in their play.
Five-star generals in concrete pits
Fight war games with noise;
While most of us regret the day
We heard the words: "Enola Gay".

Donald Armfield

Mushroom Cloud Walk

We watched it fall,
striking the sky
with an orange glow.
Stinging our eye sight,
and we blinked in terror.

Sound became a distant noise,
as our ear drums
began to bleed.

Our bodies crumbled
and we fell to our knees.
Holding the guns,
we thought would bring
us victory.

A mushroom cloud
devoured the ground
before us.
We felt our torsos disintegrate
it wiped us off the planet,
like a brush of hand
over a steamed mirror.

We never seen it coming
the cloud may have won
but it will never take
our continuing walk
in the clouds above.

Suzanne Rancourt

the dead are not dead

The grasses weep.
Thirty years ago I looked across the valley of fields
from a dorm room in Vermont.
Summer,
where has the diaphanous freedom gone?
The smooth skin of moments?

It is not
the Grasses that weep.
It is not
the voices of the dead
but their exhalation – the last breath – that flattens
the tall Grasses that
from the top floor window from which I gazed
turned silver as the underside of raspberry leaves, or Maple –
the last breath
weaves across the top of grass snake green tongue tips,
a soundless chorus of blades of grass wind made soft like
ribbon,
like a finger gracing a cheekbone or
soft flesh-hairline from breasts to belly button.
The dead
we are discussing
the dead
their final breath
the dead
exhale a vortex of flutters around the mouth, hair wisps across
the lips
shivers the meadow -
Grass Dancers.

Strider Marcus Jones

In the Name of Profit and Prophet

There's an evening coming in
Like an old friend, walking fallowed fields
Bringing rainy news.
At the town cenotaph,
He crumples and cries
For the fallen, who fall for nothing,
As the same mistakes are made
Spilling innocent blood in lost lands
In the name of Profit and Prophet.
It coughs,
And clots the light-
Like cloudy gin in battle smoke,
A grainy ghost,
Masked by music and sorcerer's spin:
The New Rome meets a fathomless faith
Destined to die in desert dust,
So some can live the dream.

Strider Marcus Jones

In Gaza

it's time to go
inside this show
of profits
and prophets-

to the motives and motifs
of tenets and beliefs,
that make a man, blow a child to bits-
in Gaza, where blood blurs bible scripts.

the gunslung
gungho,
and unsung
hero-
Goliath shelling David's ghetto into crypts,
but only Al-Jazeera shows the genocidal clips.

the currency of crime
infests divinity and time,
corrupting ideologies that blow-
through the politics, like a great and secret show.

Evan Guilford-Blake

The Invasion

We watched them dying and we were happy.

We threw our grenades and fired our bazookas. The tanks exploded. The ones who lived crawled out, their uniforms brown with sweat and red with blood; we shot at them and, as we hit them, we cheered. Women, men. Cheering, dying. Often, they did not die at once. We shot them again, in the arms and legs and genitals and waited silently. They watched each other die, they watched us watching them.

We didn't think of them as people, as human beings, with lives like ours. We knew nothing of *their* lives and didn't want to. What we knew was: We lived here, they did not. We wanted our homeland, they were invaders. Every foot of ground was land we had cleared and tilled, built our homes and shops and farms on, with our labor and our sweat. And our blood. Sometimes I think the soil seemed red from how hard the sun beat upon it. Other times it *was* red, from how hard we protected it.

Before they came our lives were hard. They have been, for generations. Usually, we had only enough to eat, at best. Sometimes -- when the rains were especially heavy or didn't come at all, or during the worst parts of summer and winter -- there was too little. We grow what we can but the soil is unforgiving of the weather and the weather has no compassion for our stomachs. There is grass for the animals so there is milk, cheese, eggs. There are rabbits and snakes. We do not grow fat but we survive. Life here has always been about surviving. I know, in some parts of the world -- theirs, I have heard -- it is about pleasures; our pleasure is from our families, our children, our parents, our history. There is a joke among my people, that our ancestors hid on the Ark and, when the flood ended, they did not wait for God to tell them to get off, they simply jumped. They didn't know any better, so they jumped here and stayed, a little place where God would pay little mind. Which He does. We have little, we know little of the world. But we have joy from those we love, we know love through their eyes and their smiles.

When I see my husband's eyes I remember that. When we fell in love we were very young; almost children. Children trust; we trusted: In ourselves, in our hope, in the future. When I married, I believed in many futures. When our first child was born I looked into her -- not just her eyes but through the skin, so pale, so thin the light shined through it, the clear brilliance of the lake under the summer sun -- and I saw her heart pounding with hope, her lungs swelling with it. That is our hope, my husband said. He touched her hand and it opened, like a flower ... like a beautiful new-bloom flower.

I have two children; and my nephew. They are still young. Not too young to know what is happening now, what has been happening these many months since *they* came again. My children don't understand. They cry when they see the uniforms; they cry out, at night, in their sleep. They have seen things a child should never see. They have seen things *you* should never see, that I don't want to see. I see them every day, since the invasion. I will describe some of them to you, you will, perhaps, understand why we cheer when they fall. Why we sit and listen -- without smiles but without remorse -- as we watch them suffer.

They have many weapons. Bombs and tanks as well as guns and grenades. The bombs and tanks destroy our homes and fields, our animals and grain. And kill us. The guns and grenades *just* kill us. Every one of us is the enemy, to their eyes. Age, sex: They don't matter. Last week, they came to the village three miles from mine. It was a small village; only a few hundred lived there. The people had only a few old rifles, knives; they used these for hunting. Sticks, machetes. My sister lived there, with her four children and her husband -- an old man, over fifty, with a crutch.

They killed them all, except my ten year old nephew. He hid from them and they did not find him. But he saw. First they killed the youngest -- she was four. The others were bound and forced to watch. They killed the seven year old, the twelve year old, my sister, then my brother-in-law. My nephew who escaped said they asked, every time they raised the gun or knife or bayonet: where are the weapons. My family answered: there are no weapons. They did not believe that, so they killed them. The children were shot in the head. My sister and brother-in-law were cut -- no; carved -- open. Slowly, my nephew said, with their mouths gagged as they were sliced so they could not scream from the pain. And after each cut the gag was removed, so they could be asked, again, the same question they could not answer. They left them, unburied. Then they burned everything, to the ground. When I saw it there was nothing but ash. You could not even tell what had been human. My nephew held my hand. He wept. I wept.

Before they came I saw so much beauty here. The mountains, they rise through the clouds, when the sun rises over them they are gold with the snow and stone of the peaks. The rocks are black, spare saplings and old, huge trees struggle among them. At night the sky is clear and black, the stars are white. It is still beautiful but I rarely notice that now. There is too much else I *must* notice: sudden movement, tracks in the mud, fires in the dark, camouflage. There is too much to listen for, too; once, I listened for the music in the wind, and from the birds, from the songs we sang, from our pipes, our drums.

Now, listening -- for their small sounds, their language, their laughter -- is what comes before we attack. We attack and run. It is the only way we can fight; the terrain is difficult: we know it, they do not. We travel in small troops, carrying little, but there are many of us and we are good shots. We have learned to listen; and we have learned silence. That has been hard. We are a joyful people, we express what we feel in shouts and songs and claps. We dance. Even now, I dance; it is not from joy, but it *is* a way to remember joy.

We do not need music to dance. Dancing is a celebration, it comes from within, where there is always music. Our drums and pipes, they make music too; but it is different, that is the music of our country. *This* music is the music of our souls. It is the language we speak to ourselves. The other is for speaking to the rest of the world.

The rest of the world knows as little of us as we do of them. They read in their newspapers: there is a war in a far off place. They see pictures on their televisions. I do not think they are indifferent, but our problems are not their problems; we matter less to them than they matter to themselves. We are foreign to them, just as invasion is foreign. We have been invaded, repeatedly, for centuries; we have, always, driven the invaders away. A people defends its land, its people, its history, its way of life. Those who come say there is something better, they can make our lives better if we will live their way of life. But what is better? To live as you have always lived, to believe and pray and celebrate as you have always done, to accept change as *you* create it; or to live with values you do not know or recognize, and change because you are forced to? That is the true foreignness, to have your nature dissolved by the acids of other cultures, to have children and grandchildren taught ways and meanings which are not born of the traditions you yourself know. "Different" is not better. -- We change; we must: change is inevitable. But what we have *been*, that cannot change. The invaders, they would displace that with what *they* have been, they want to remake our hearts as they want to remake our land, our economy, our government.

There were invasions when I was a child. My parents told us of the invaders that came when *they* were children, just as their parents and grandparents had told each generation before.

Invading this land is a tradition, I think. A rite of passage: Our neighbors' children come of age by stepping onto our soil, rifle on shoulder, and killing. My grandfather said our troubles are the will of God, that God would have us struggle in this life to remember that it is the next one that matters. Which is, I suppose, why so many of us go on to the next one so soon. I wonder what those in the next life think when they look down to us -- are they saddened, anxious, annoyed, infuriated by what they see? Are they scornful -- do they "look down" on us as well as at us? Do they plead with God for mercy, or smile as God raises a hand -- or does not raise a hand -- and we suffer?

God would have us suffer, it is said. That I do not understand. *God*, like the invaders, I do not understand. Perhaps God is beyond human understanding, as the clerics say, but I cannot accept that: we are, all of us, in body and thought, in deed and in action, the spawn of God's intention. If it is God's *intention* that we are, continually, to conflict, then we are pointless: conflict is the annihilation of the value of life; *harmony* is the creation of its value. I am not so naive or immature to believe in the perfection of the world, but I know I would rather love than kill. I believe our people believe that, too. The invaders do not -- they would not *come* here if they did not want to kill, more than anything, for they know, must know, that without killing they cannot conquer. So I believe God is like the foreigners: our problems are not God's problems, God does not - interfere to help Mankind; not to hinder Mankind. We are objects of study: a scientific experiment: its integrity would be compromised by divine intervention.

Therefore I do not *worship* God. I believe in One, a deity which created the Universe, One which *possesses* the power to destroy any part of it. But I do not worship, because the - indifference of such a deity does not deserve adoration.

What I adore is life. Without the invasion life is full, it is rich, it is the sight of the deserts from the top of the mountains: broad and endless, an horizon that is dark and light and gray. It is the harsh earth, it is the music of the moon's radiance. In peaceful times, before they came again, we lived life. Now we live only war, the battles: Against them, for our survival. For our homeland.

They watched us dying and they were happy.

They threw grenades and fired bazookas. Our tanks exploded. Most of us died inside them. Those in mine survived. I crawled out, behind the others; our uniforms were drenched with sweat and blood. Somehow -- in the fire and smoke, I think -- they did not see me crawl away. I hid, in a rock pile. The ones they saw, they shot. I heard cries and moans, and cheers. Women, men. Cheering, dying. Some did not die at once. There were more shots, my comrades cried, but no other sounds, no words. Finally the cries stopped. I heard boots, and voices rasping their language. I waited, the boots and voices grew softer. When they were gone I crawled out. They had left the bodies there, on the ground. They were shot in the arms, legs, and genitals. They waited while we died. They watched us and waited, silently.

They are not human beings, with souls like ours. All we know of them is what we see: they destroy, they have no mercy. We would have peace; they do not allow it. We come here because they threaten us: do not pass through this nation, they tell us, do not use these roads to cross the mountains; or we will attack. We have goods we must deliver; there is no other route. So we take our trucks and they attack them. Before there were trucks, they attacked our carts and wagons. And that was not enough. On our border there are villages where they come, at night, they set fires, they destroy the grain, the shops, the forests. Many are killed. More are left without food, clothing, homes.

My homeland is a large country. We are farmers, fishermen, carpenters, weavers. Poor people, almost all. But we are proud: we have made our land provide for us. We have raised food on soil that is too dry, too hard, too-much used. We have woven wool into scarves and vests of such beauty they are treasured for generations. Tables, chairs, bowls that are art, shaped from the wood of our many trees; in the summer the green of their boughs reaches almost to heaven. We can stand below the shimmer of their color, see the sparkle below the hidden sun, a legend says that God has given this part of the world a sky of emeralds. When they are hungry the children stand and wait for them to fall. "We will have food," they say, "when the sky rains green."

Until we came here, I had never left my homeland. I have been away a year; I miss it. This land is mountains and deserts; ours is plains and forests. Theirs is old and slow; ours is young and eager. Their people are angry and cold. Ours are joyous and warm. We are filled with the hunger to learn of the wonders life has to offer. These people have no wonder. I have seen them stare at the world, as if it were a blank slate on which they have no need to create.

But creating is the meaning of life. Creating *is* life: I have two children. My husband and I created them, and we create them again each day. There is such - extraordinary beauty in their faces, their eyes: they look at me and in them, I see the world as it could be -- a vast openness, a vast hope, a vast empty canvas to be filled with the dreams my husband and I can paint upon them.

155

My children write to me. They say: I miss you. They say: I cannot sleep when you are gone. They say: when will you come home so my sister will not cry because you do not sing us songs or carry us on your shoulders or kiss us when we are sad. I write to them: I miss you. I say: I cannot sleep when I am without you. I say: I kiss you every morning and every night, I walk this land with you on my shoulders and on my heart with the longing I have to be with you again. My children should not be without their mother. I know their nightmares; I had the same ones as a child, when *my* mother came here to face these people. I had the same fears.

But I am here. I am here because it is my duty; not just to my country, it is my duty because among the villages on our border is one where my uncle lived. I was fourteen when I saw that village the last time; when I saw the empty sockets where my uncle's eyes had been, the stake upon which his twelve year old daughter was impaled, because they had no food, no livestock, left to give to the invaders who demanded them. Those are things a child should never see. Those are things no one should ever see. They cannot be forgotten. They should not be. I still think of them. I weep now, as I did then.

I weep, too, because here I have killed children. These people, sex, age do not matter to them: the children are taught to fight, they hide, they shoot at us, they run. Old men hide bullets in the hollows of their crutches. Young girls hide explosives in the heads of their dolls. They deny it, but we know they are there; we have found them time and time again. Last week, we --- I - killed three children; we killed their mother, their father, in a small village. There *were* weapons there, but they would not tell us where they were hidden. We burned everything; after, we found a pile of rocks; there were grenades and plastics beneath them. *We did not want to kill them.* But these people, of this village, had killed so many of our comrades.

We could not let them keep their weapons. We could not let them live. This land is filled with our blood. I walk through it; everywhere there are reddish-brown stains, everywhere the scent of copper.

Before I left my land, I walked throughout my village. There was so much beauty to be seen. Narrow streets smelling of morning, coffees and baking and firewood-smoke. Music, there was so much music, fiddles and flutes and spinets praising the notes. Children dancing. Children shouting. Children dancing and shouting at the joy of sunlight. I taught my daughters to dance -- we dance together. Now, here, I dance to recall that, though I dance alone.

We do not need music to dance. Dancing is in our souls, we are born to *that* music, that only we can hear. There is music we play for the world; but I contain *our* music. Even here, *even here*, I can feel it, my daughters', my husband's, my peoples'.

The world doesn't know that music. The world doesn't know *us*. They read in their newspapers: there are people who must go to war. They know *of* our struggles, but they do not care about them. Our struggles are not theirs. Our way of life is not theirs, just as it is not the way of this land. But in this land they think their way is better, they would prevent change, our own and theirs; but there must be change: without change a nation does not grow. A people cannot live in the past. They do not see that, they do not recognize that "different" is not worse, that the lives they live isolate them from us, from the world. To embrace change is to accept the world. To deny it is to deny nature.

Sometimes I am afraid. For my life, but more for my children: our people have fought here for centuries. I think *we* are children until we step onto this soil, rifle in hand. Then we kill and come of age. My grandmother said one must be a woman to kill. The world, I think, needs more children and fewer women. Children can have faith: in themselves, in the world, in God. I had that, once. Now, seeing this, *being* this, faith and God are beyond belief. If God wants us to kill, to die in the pursuit of death, God is cruel. It is cruel, to annihilate life, to trample its value like an unnoticed wild flower. I am not so naive that I believe in the perfection of humanity, but I know I would rather love than take lives. I believe our people believe that, too. These people do not -- if they did not *want* to kill they would welcome us, let us welcome them, as neighbors. So I believe God, in His cruelty, allows the killing, shakes His head as it happens, but says, as the world says: theirs are not my problems.

I cannot worship God. I believe in One, a deity which created the Universe. But I do not worship it, because such cruelty does not deserve consecration.

What I consecrate is life. When the invasion is over life will be full. I will see the pale dry-yellow plains of my homeland, its green horizons, hear the bitter wind and the sweet splash of stones into a stream. I will hear the music of my children's smiles. I will, again, live life. In peaceful times, before I came, we lived life. Now we live only war, the battles: against them, for our survival. For our homeland.

G.L. Helm

Lessons of War

22 May, 2005

Remember—
The glory fades,
The stench of battle lingers.
The copper smell of blood,
The shit and vomit reek of pierc'ed bowel
The soldiers' corpse miasma,
Lingers.
When spring warms the earth,
The carrion birds still gather
In forests
Where Romans battled Britons.
They gather still
At Antitem
At Verdun
At St. Lo
At Iwo Jima
At DaNang
At Faluja.
Remember.
The glory fades
The stench remains.

Jodie English

Psalm of our Longing

First light brings rain —
patterned, steady
on our flat faces,
our stooped shoulders,
our lawns cut green.
Rain sends minnows of dust
down the hearse glass, rain
soaks flag-draped
coffins, rain slaps dirt
onto acres of caskets,
the minnows drown
in the turbulent sea.

Suzanne Rancourt

A Bridge of Social Renaissance

a string of grottos
a rank of empty eye sockets
a reverse negative of blackened teeth
a harmonica played as a bridge by fleeing feet
from mountain range to lowlands
away from bandits, pirates, insurgent shadows
bleeding into meadows, an ink stain blotting peace

the bridge was intended to be a structure of beauty
a gesture of connecting two lands together
an exchange of trust not
the black keys on a piano
playing chords of dissonance and sharp contrasts

Author Bios

J. J. Steinfeld has written both short fiction and novel-length fiction, plays, and poetry. He is the recipient of numerous awards including the Norma Epstein Award (1979), the Okanagan Short Fiction Award (1984, 1990), and Great Canadian Novella Competition (1986), the Toronto Jewish Congress Book Committee Creative Writing Award (1990), and the Award of Distinguished Contribution to the Literary Arts on Prince Edward Island (2003). His playwriting has won him awards from the Theatre Prince Edward Island Playwriting Competition. He has three published poetry collections. The latest was published in August of last year and deals with the impact of his parents' Holocaust experience on their lives as well as his. It is titled *Identity Dreams and Memory Sounds.*

Raymond Walker has a diploma in Journalism Administration and a B.A. in English Literature. He has worked as a writer, photographer and editor. He is now living in Vancouver and concentrating on writing fiction, which is what he really wanted to do before getting sidetracked by a journalism career. He has had short stories published in *Descant* and *Spinetingler* magazines as well as creative non-fiction in *The Globe and Mail.*

Among his recent publications are his short story "A Special Occasion", which can be read at *Spinetingler Magazine*: http://www.spinetinglermag.com/2015/04/13/fiction-a-special-occasion-by-raymond-walker/ and "Christ's Sad

Eyes", which can be read at *One Throne Magazine*: http://www.onethrone.com/#!christs-sad-eyes/cx28

Neil Davies currently lives in the northwest of England with his wife and two children. Any spare time he can find he spends writing horror and science fiction.

He has four works published by small presses:

The Midnight Hour (short story collection) – Screaming Dreams (2007)
"Hard Winter" (science fiction/horror short story) – Eternal Press (2009)
Hard Winter: The Novel (science fiction/horror novel) – Omnium Gatherum (2013)
The Village Witch (horror novel) – Omnium Gatherum (2015)

He also has some self-published work. You can find all his published work on Amazon.

For more information please visit his official website - http://www.nwdavies.co.uk

email: neil@nwdavies.co.uk
Facebook: https://www.facebook.com/nwdavies
Twitter: https://twitter.com/nwdavies
LinkedIn: https://www.linkedin.com/pub/neil-davies/14/b48/a6a

Alexis Liosatos is based in Wales, UK. He is a writer, artist and teacher. He has spent most of his working life in the arts, as a magazine and book illustrator, a computer games character designer, a freelance photographer, and a portrait painter. He has covered subjects ranging from lightweight romantic fiction to the blackest depths of the Cthulhu   Mythos.

'The Man Who Collected Dali' is Alexis's first published story. It draws upon his knowledge of art and his understanding of the dark alchemy that sometimes goes into the making of a painting. The historical backdrop informing the story is as accurately researched as possible.

Alexis would like to thank Martijn Albers from the Museum Boijmans Van Beuningen, Rotterdam for supplying information about the movements of a certain painting of Salvador Dali's across the borders of Europe. One day, Alexis intends to stand in front of this painting and see it with his own eyes.

Evan Guilford-Blake writes prose, plays and poetry for adults and children. His short story collection *American Blues* (nominated for a Georgia Author of the Year award) was published last year by Holland House. Evan (and the book) will be among those featured at the 2015 Decatur Book Festival -- the largest independent book festival in the US -- over Labor Day Weekend, concurrent with the publication of his novel *Animation* by Deeds Publishing. Penguin   published   his   novel *Noir(ish).*   This fall, Rooster and Pig will release his children's novel *The Bluebird Prince,* and Verto Publishing will publish *Love & Loss & Love,* another book of his short stories, in January. His work has also appeared in more than 50 journals and anthologies, and he has stories in several soon-to-be released anthologies and magazines. His prose has won 21 competitions; his plays have won 42 awards and have been produced internationally.   Thirty-one   are   published. Information   about   his   published prose   is   available at http://www.amazon.com/-/e/B009CC554I, and about his plays at https://www.treepress.org/playwright/evan-guilford-blake

Read synopses of and dialogue samples from his plays at the New Play Exchange and Tree Press Facebook: https://www.facebook.com/evan.guilfordblake Twitter: @EJBplaywright

Eric Paul Shaffer is author of five books of poetry, including Lāhaina Noon; Living at the Monastery, Working in the Kitchen; and Portable Planet. More than 400 of his poems have appeared in more than 200 local and national reviews as well as many in Australia, Canada, England, Ireland, Japan, New Zealand, Scotland, and Wales. Shaffer has received a number of local literary awards, including the 2002 Elliot Cades Award, a 2006 Ka Palapala Po'okela Book Award for Lāhaina Noon, and the 2009 James M. Vaughan Award for Poetry. He teaches composition, literature, and creative writing at Honolulu Community College.

His poems "April Fool: A Minor Event on L-Day, April 1, 1945, Okinawa, with no apologies to history" and "Voice of Stone: June 16, 1996, Peace Day on Okinawa, for #30571" appear in *In the Trenches* and were previously published in 2000 by Leaping Dog Press in *Portable Planet*.

You can find some of his published work at the Leaping Dog Press website: http://www.leapingdogpress.com/authors/eric-paul-shaffer/

Some of his online poem publications can be found at the following links: The Sun Magazine http://thesunmagazine.org/issues/428/illumination

Slate
http://www.slate.com/articles/arts/poem/2007/01/sitting_in_the_last_of_sunset_listening_to_guests_within.html
Southword   Journal   (Ireland)
http://www.munsterlit.ie/Southword/Contributors/shaffe r_ericpaul.html
Rattle
http://www.rattle.com/poetry/the-word-swallower-by-eric-paul-shaffer/
Terrain.org
http://www.terrain.org/poetry/21/shaffer.htm
Weber: The   Contemporary   West
http://weberstudies.weber.edu/archive/archive%20D%20Vol.%2021.2-25.2/Vol.%2025.2/Eric%20Paul%20Shaffer%20Poe.htm

Donald Armfield started reading ritually six years ago. There wasn't a place he was seen without a book in his hand. His first publication came when he meant some cool cats in the Bizarro world. "Walking After Midnight" published by Rooster Republic was his first trip into the world of writing. Currently he has tackled many different sub-genres and has made a small name for his self. His first novella was published by Riot Forge at the end of 2014 "Hung Hounds" a sci-fi romp of laughing time travel, apocalyptic adventure of bizarre happenings.

He has also been published by James Ward Kirk Fiction, J Ellington Ashton Press, Fireside Press and Dynatox Ministries, to name a few. He has two poems published with Hash 'N Pumpkins blog. On the horizon he has his first poetry collection coming out later this year and a few other projects. Check him out.......

https://www.facebook.com/donald.armfield

http://www.amazon.com/Donald-
Armfield/e/B00P2ZJLOY/ref=sr_ntt_srch_lnk_1?qid=14
34588952&sr=8-1

Lemmy Rushmore is a mechanic by trade and father of three who occasionally dares dabble in the world of words. Until recently unpublished, his pieces touch on many topics, but tend to lean toward the darker side of those things encountered daily. Ranging from emotionally dark to horror, some of his work can be seen in the anthologies We are Dust and Shadow, Demonic Possession, and No Sight for the Saved, which features the superbly dark art of Niall Parkinson. All have been released by James Ward Kirk Publishing and are now available. His newest published work appears in Between the Walls, the result of a collaboration with artist Niall Parkinson. All of Lemmy's works can be found on Amazon.

Strider Marcus Jones is a poet, law graduate and ex-civil servant from England with deep Celtic roots in Ireland and Wales. A member of The Poetry Society, his five published books of poetry (http://www.lulu.com/spotlight/stridermarcusjones1) are modern, traditional, mythical, sometimes erotic, surreal and metaphysical. When not writing, he can be heard playing his saxophone and clarinet (just ask his neighbours).

His poetry has been published most recently in The Screech Owl, Catweazle and The Gambler magazines; Vagabonds: Anthology Of The Mad, mgv2 Publishing Anthology, Killer Whale Journal, The Huffington Post USA and Writer's Ezine.

John De Herrera is a writer/artist/activist who lives and works in Santa Barbara, California. He is the author of The

Kingsnake in the Sun, Hamlet/Macbeth: Translations, and is currently working on his second novel.

Christopher S. Nelson serves as US Army Cavalry Scout and former Tanker, with multiple deployments to the Republic of Korea, Kuwait, and Iraq. He is a Bronze Star recipient for actions performed during Operation Iraqi Freedom 07-09 while serving as a Scout Platoon Sergeant in Mosul, Iraq. Currently, Sergeant First Class Nelson trains Scout and Infantry Recon Platoons at the National Training Center in Fort Irwin. He lives with his wife, son, and Queensland Heeler and spends his free time adventuring as far from the Mojave with his family as possible. His second craft is music and when not hiking or exploring he can be found in his library, playing guitar. His only other interest at this time is raising scorpions and tarantulas, though he is currently on orders for Alaska and this arachnid rescue fixation is now on hold. As a writer, CS Nelson has works published in US and Canadian presses. He also edits for Booktrope's Forsaken Imprint and enjoys working with writers on projects in an editorial and plot-to-destroy-the-world capacity. You can find a list of many of his works on his website, www.nelsoncs.com. In addition to the works listed there he has had three stories published in anthologies by J. Ellington Ashton Press - "Bloat" (Axes of Evil II: Rise of the Metal Gods), "Plug" (Chunks: A Barfzarro Anthology), and "Markets" (Suburban Secrets: A Neighborhood of Nightmares). You can also find him on Twitter at csnelson_ext849.

Roger Cowin currently lives in Centerville, IN. He has been writing and publishing poetry for three decades. Recently he has been branching out into fiction where he blends his love of horror with satire and humor. He is the author of the poetry collections, "Passing Through

Darkness & Other Poems" and "Succulent Flesh," published by JWK Fiction. His forthcoming collection of short stories "Old Scratch's Book of Peculiar Tales" will be published by JWK Fiction later this year.

David S. Pointer has military or war-themed poems published around the horn. David's most recent military poetry publication is "The Childhood Psychology of Militaristic Assent" at "Military Experience & the Arts" online at Eastern Kentucky University. His work "MPs, Snipers and Crime" will be reissued by Writing Knights Press and sold on Amazon.com in the near future. Links to some of his other publications can be found below.

Beyond Shark Tag Bay
Sundrenched Nanosilver
Backyard Sniper Training
Terror Train

Stuart Keane is rounding out his first year as a published author. Featuring numerous times in several horror anthologies during 2014, he is finishing
some short story obligations before writing his second novel, Boys, in 2015. Currently, you can find Stuartpublished in a number of anthologies, including Dead Harvest, Cellar III: Animals/Hell II: Citizens, Terror Train, Floppy Shoes Apocalypse, Rejected for Content: Splattergore, and Journals of Horror: Found Fiction. He has also released novellas The Customer is Always... and Charlotte, as well as his debut novel, All or Nothing. All books are available on Amazon.com. Read more about the author at www.stuartkeane.com. He currently resides in Ipswich, UK, with his wife and an unhealthy caffeine addiction.

Donald Jacob Uitvlugt lives on neither coast of the United States, but mostly in a haunted memory palace of his own design. His short fiction has previously appeared in numerous print and online venues, including Necrotic Tissue and the Wily Writers podcast, as well as the anthologies A Fistful of Horrors and the charity anthology New Sun Rising: Stories for Japan. He strives to write what he calls "haiku fiction," stories that are small in scale but big in impact.If you enjoyed "Good Dog," you can let him know at his webpage http://haikufiction.blogspot.com or via Twitter @haikufictiondju.

Angi Holden is a freelance writer, whose work includes prize winning adult & children's poetry, short stories & flash fictions, published in online and print anthologies. She brings a wide range of personal experience to her writing, from a nomadic Forces childhood, through university and subsequent qualification as an accountant, to later study in 3D design and creative writing. Her family are central to her life and her research into her family history has been a significant influence on her writing.

D. Thomas Minton recently traded a warm tropical island for the Pacific Northwest of the continental USA, where he now lives a short walk from vineyards and an alpaca farm. When not writing, he gets paid to "play" in the ocean, travel to remote places, and help communities conserve coral reefs. His fiction has been published in Asimov's, Lightspeed, andDaily Science Fiction and his idle ramblings hold court at dthomasminton.com. His story "Portraits from the Shadow" appears in *In the Trenches* and originally appeared in Intergalactic Medicine Show.

Tom D. Nolan lives in Birmingham, UK. His writing to date has been primarily for performance with work produced on tv, radio and stage. He recently placed second in the 2014 Story Pros screenwriting contest.

Suzanne S. Rancourt, MS, MFA, CASAC-T, and past Editor of Bluestreak: Journal of Military Poetry. She is a multi-modal Expressive Arts Therapist, Consultant, Educator. An armed services veteran with service time in both the Marine Corps and the Army, recipient of the Native Writers' Circle of the Americas First Book Award, her work has been published in The Muddy River Review, Ginosko Journal, and The Journal of Military Experience vol 2 and vol 3, Chiron Review #98, and Four Winds Literary Magazine. Ms. Rancourt is Abenaki, (Northeast woodland) born and raised in the mountains of West Central Maine. Suzanne remains involved with Military Experience and Arts and was a presenter and MEA 1 and 2. She is an Amherst Writers' & Artist affiliate and is an AWA Writing workshop facilitator. For more information on Ms. Rancourt's Expressive Arts philosophy: www.expressive-arts.com

G. L. Helm has been writing for forty years. He has traveled around the world with his long suffering Air Force wife. They raised two sons while living in Spain, Germany, and Italy, and in less exotic places like Virginia and Indiana. He now lives in Lancaster Ca. Helm has written four novels. He has also written reams of short stories which have been published in anthologies around the world.

Jodie English is an attorney in private practice in Indianapolis, handling serious felonies, including death penalty cases - the latter at times as a trial defender, a mentor in post-conviction and, most recently, as a mitigation specialist and jury consultant. Jodie has taught criminal defense lawyers in twenty-seven states and was part of a team invited to Moscow to facilitate the Russians' transition from three-judge panels to juries. She completed her MFA at Butler University in 2014. In her spare time, Jodie writes poetry and creative nonfiction, jogs, kayaks, and reads. She is both a lover and a fighter and is enriched by her Quaker faith, her children and daily meditation and journaling.

Matthew Wilson has had over 150 appearances in such places as Horror Zine, Star*Line, Spellbound, Illumen, Apokrupha Press, Gaslight Press, Sorcerers Signal and many more. He is currently editing his first novel and can be contacted on twitter @matthew94544267.

Eve Gaal, M.A.(Human Behavior) was born in Boston, but her parents saw the evils of war in Europe. Though brilliant engineers and proud American citizens, their memories were sad, their souls forever scarred. Her parents' stories and their unending pain led Eve to Steve, her husband of 23 years who came from the same war-torn nation as her parents. Except Steve was a tiny baby shuffled into bomb shelters who also grew up dreaming of peace—hoping to find love. Months after arriving in the States, Steve joined the U.S. Army. Eve was a toddler banging on her toy typewriter. Someday, the grief she heard from her parents and the agony described by Steve would manifest itself in her writing. "The title of this anthology describes my life," said Eve from her home in California. "Even though I've never experienced the atrocities of conflict, I've heard so many horrific stories and dodged the effects of PTSD my entire life that I have a serious emotional connection with those who have suffered from war." Find more about Eve at www.evegaal.com

www.ingramcontent.com/pod-product-compliance
Lightning Source LLC
Chambersburg PA
CBHW070921130626
46555CB00001B/224